LITTLE GEMS

TIGER'S EYE

2019

ROMANCE
WRITERS
of Australia

Tiger's eye 2019: Little Gems Anthology

Anthology of Short Stories published by Romance Writers of Australia

Inc © 2019

Ebook format: 978-0-6485877-1-2

Print format: 978-0-6485877-0-5

Little Gems Coordinator: Michelle Diener

Cover design by Lana Pecherczyk

Edited by Kim Lambert

OTHER LITTLE GEMS ANTHOLOGIES

Diamond 2012

Sapphire 2013

Moonstone 2014

Peridot 2015

Sunstone 2016

Onyx 2017

Jade 2018

LITTLE GEMS

TIGER'S EYE

Short Story Anthology

2019

CONTENTS

FOREWORD

Sixteen stories, all based around the one gemstone – Tiger Eye.

And all of them completely different.

What aspects of Tiger Eye will our authors use to build their tales?

It's amazing colours, ranging from reddish-brown through to gold, like the flashing eye of a tiger?

It's beautiful silky lustre?

How it is mined in South Africa or here in Australia?

Or will they choose to look at the metaphysical?

The Egyptians used the stone in the eyes of their deity statues, giving it the symbolic task of seeing everything, knowing everything.

Ancient Roman soldiers carried Tiger Eye into battle for good fortune.

And today, crystal healers advise you to use Tiger Eye for confidence, courage, and strength of will.

So, what have the best of the best of short story writers in RWA come up with this year?

Whatever it is, you are assured of a happy ending to each of these romantic beauties.

I am so pleased to be able to present to you our newest Little Gems Anthology, Tiger Eye.

Bree Vreedenburgh

RWA President, 2019

1

ONE AND DONE

CHELSEA LOCKE

*R*egrets? Hell no!

What a night! Jane Beatrix Bryce, when you decide to shake up your dreary non-existent encounters with the opposite sex and then proceed to indulge in various carnal adventures over the space of one crazy night with a sizable dirty blond, green-eyed sex god, you most certainly go right off the reservation sweetheart.

"Are you awake?" queried the deep tingle-inducing voice.

"I'm awake, the real question is why?" Jane queried while luxuriating in the luscious lethargy that follows truly exceptional fucking.

"I have to be somewhere sooner rather than later, and I didn't want to just leave." A lazy smile spread across his face, and those hypnotic eyes were now twinkling.

She returned his smile. "Where do you need to be so early on a Saturday morning, Michael?"

"Nothing serious, just a day where I have to be somewhere at a stupidly early time." Lazily he rolled onto his back and, moving both hands down to her hips, he very comfortably lifted her, so she was sitting on his thighs. "Last night was fantastic."

Jane stretched and nodded in agreement. "I think fantastic is an understatement, I say epic." Leaning down, Jane brushed aside his messy hair and placed a gentle kiss on his forehead.

Looking intently at her, he slowly butterflied his fingers on the swell of her breast and she responded in kind by grazing a hand over his chest and down over his splendid toned stomach. She was tempted to continue down that track of dark hair, but she sensed that time was against them. They smiled sleepily at each other, almost reluctant to say anything for fear it would finally end their agreed one and only night together. He reached and captured her slim wrist and stroked the delicate silver bangle.

"I love this stone," he commented. "Do you know what it is, sweetheart?"

Jane shook her head and smiled "No idea, I bought it at the local markets a few weeks ago." She looked down at the stone and the long blunt-tipped fingers that had captured her wrist. "I just fell in love with the stone - such a dark, rich, lustrous brown with these vivid slashes of yellow through it. To be honest, I had never seen this type of stone before." Her face lit up with obvious amusement. "Plus, the stall owner was a fabulous salesman, and somehow, someway, he convinced me that this pretty bangle and I belong together." Jane grinned down at Michael. "Pretty crazy eh?"

"Not at all," he replied, "the stone is tiger's eye." His deep voice and touches were sending delicious shivers through Jane. He continued, knowing the effect his touch was having on them both. "My Nana loves the stone, and it has real sentimental importance to my family."

"How so?"

Before Michael could respond, the pre-dawn night was disturbed by the loud and very intrusive sound of Gwen Stefani singing about what a bad girl she was. He smiled apologetically "I have to take this. Yeah Stacey." He listened intently.

Jane watched him, while chastising herself for being a tiny bit jealous of Stacey, who had interrupted their early morning idyll. Was Stacey the reason he had to leave so early, she wondered? *OK, Jane shut this possessive suspicious thinking down right now. This night was all about one and done.*

"I hear you and yes, I know I'm late." Sighing softly, he continued, "I do know what day it is, ease up on the attitude please, and I will see you when I get there."

Slowly he set the phone down and lifted his body up to kiss her. His face was alight with humour. "Sorry about that - Stacey can get worked up. I know you were insistent that it was to be just one night, but we have some magic chemistry bubbling away here." He again reached for her wrist and, turning it over, pressed a warm kiss against the inside. "I really think we should do some further investigation." He offered one of the perfect smiles which had so captured Jane's attention when she'd first seen him leaning against a pool table, laughing with what was apparently a group of close friends.

Jane knew, there and then, that this man was dangerous to her perfectly laid plans of avoiding all emotional entanglements. Time to shut this down, whatever this was.

She exhaled. "I don't think so Michael, in fact, even second dates are rare for me." She smiled and said in a firm voice, "No let's not spoil a beautiful night by trying to make it something more." A slightly sad feeling washed through her as she realised that she would never meet her Mister One and Done again. She mentally slammed that pity party down and tumbled down beside him, peppering him with tiny, flirtatious goodbye kisses.

"Better head off," she teased, "before Stacey becomes even more agitated."

CƷ℮Ͻ

Jane fastened her stylish, broad brimmed hat, then stood back and studied her reflection. She was delighted with the red and orange fit and flare dress which floated out in a pretty feminine circle around her long, lean, tanned legs. Her father was due to arrive at any moment for their day at the races, and she knew that this determination to look stylish and perfect was all aimed at avoiding criticism from her father, David Bryce.

Theirs was an uncomfortable father-daughter relationship, due to her father's propensity to divorce and marry at regular intervals, Meg being the fifth Mrs Bryce in residence at Casa Bryce. Was it any wonder she avoided second dates and was distrustful with gorgeous early risers like Michael, mused Jane? She wondered, once again, just what hold the mysterious Stacey had over Michael, and followed that swiftly by once again chiding herself for this unexpected jealousy and possessiveness. A short time later saw Jane settling in the hire car, next to her father.

"You're looking very presentable Jane."

Jane smiled quizzically at her father "Damned by faint praise so early in our day together, Dad."

"Oh, honey you look lovely, sometimes I can be tactless without realising it," he explained ruefully.

Jane softened and decided to work a little harder to connect with her father, who was obviously wanting to spend the day with his eldest daughter. "Meg not joining us today?"

"No, not today. I wanted a day just with my beautiful daughter."

"Me too, it will be fun to have a father and daughter day together. Plus, the bonus of a day in the best corporate suite." Father and daughter looked at each other and Jane continued. "Today is all about us, quality French champagne, backing winners and, of course," she added, "delicious food." She looked across at her Father. "What's not to love?" She flashed a quick smile in his direction. "Do you think they will serve those yummy little-smoked salmon canapes again? That would make the day perfect."

An hour later saw her father's driver deliver them to Randwick Racecourse and Jane was relaxed and cheerful. Her father was very intent on tracking down a highly successful trainer who was reluctant to take David Bryce on as a client. Jane could well understand why the trainer would be hesitant, David Bryce had the reputation of being a mercurial owner, often swinging the pendulum in extremes from lavish praise to blistering denouncements of skill and ability.

Arriving in the suite, Jane looked around for familiar faces, intending to ease away from her father and maintain the relaxed peace they were currently enjoying. Accepting a flute of champagne, she wandered over to the large panoramic window, while surveying her fellow guests, when into the room strode Mister One and Done. Jane somehow resisted spluttering quality French champagne. As he moved into the suite, engaging with all in his path, Jane swiftly slipped through the many groups of guests, making her way to someplace unobtrusive. Heart pounding, she wondered why he was here, and where was the early-calling Stacey. Spying a woman sitting alone in a cosy corner, Jane walked towards the smiling woman. The woman indicated to Jane to take the deep plush lounge next to her.

"Hello I'm Barbara Wright, and like you, I'm distancing myself from all that hullabaloo."

Jane smiled in greeting, introduced herself and asked, "Can I organise a glass of champagne for you, Barbara?"

"No need," announced a voice that, not twelve hours ago, was whispering wicked words and suggestions in her ear. With a start, Jane looked up and saw that her efforts to escape had been pointless.

Barbara laughed with delight. "Mikey, what a darling boy you are. Come and meet Jane who, just like me, is wanting to escape the madding crowd."

"Hello Jane, lovely to meet you," he drawled, with a teasing smile.

Jane could scarcely believe this was the same man who had tumbled out of her bed early this morning, now replaced by a perfectly groomed, booted and suited man with his thick blond hair slicked back, a tad too long and curling at the collar of his crisp white shirt.

Jane returned his smile with a mischievous grin. "Delighted to meet you, Mikey."

"Please call me Mike or Michael. My darling Nana still sees

me as a five-year-old." Turning away, reluctantly, from Jane he said, "So, Nana, ready to come with me down to ringside to see your horse?"

Barbara turned to Jane. "My horse," she chuckled with amusement. "What my handsome grandson means is that he has named the horse after my favourite stone."

"Let me guess," Jane jumped in. "Tiger's Eye."

Barbara gasped. "How did you know?" Jane immediately realised that she had walked right into a trap and was unsure how to explain her knowledge.

At that moment, her father barrelled into the conversation. "Michael, I've been wanting to catch you for a chat about training Prince Diaz."

Jane rolled her eyes in amusement at her father's rude intrusion, but he had saved her from explaining her tiger's eye faux pas.

"Jane, how do you know Michael?"

"We just met." Jane turned laughing eyes in Barbara's direction. Their peaceful corner had become very busy. "Dad, can I introduce Michael's grandmother? Barbara Wright."

David leaned across the low table to take Barbara's hand. "It's a pleasure to meet you, Barbara. I met your husband many times over the years - an exceptional man and trainer. George had a real gift with horses, and it appears your grandson has been blessed with the gift as well." He paused as he patted Barbara's hand in a consoling gesture. "I was so sad to hear of his death and I'm sorry for your loss."

Barbara smiled. "Thank you, David. Yes, we miss him every

day."

For a moment, the four were silent, unsure what was to happen next. Barbara stepped up. "Mikey, I really can't be bothered to go down to the ring, why not take Jane with you." Turning to Jane she said, "Jane, you will love it. As you have probably guessed, Mikey is the trainer. He will be giving last minute instructions to the jockey, and answering a few queries from the media and, let's be honest, he is going to look considerably more handsome with you beside him." Turning to Jane's father, Barbara suggested that he sit with her to watch the race and then, when her grandson returned, he could chat with him.

Michael did not waste a moment. He reached for Jane and pulled her quickly to her feet. "Sounds like a great idea Nana." As he tucked Jane's hand through his arm, he checked one last time, "You're sure you don't want to join us?" Barbara's only response was to wave them on their way with a smile and a wink.

As they walked out of the suite, Jane could not resist stating the obvious. "You train racehorses."

"I do," he responded, "and I have to say, I was not happy having to leave you so early this morning, I was cursing my chosen career."

She laughed. "To be honest I was cursing you for making my Saturday start so early."

"Sweetheart, the moment I left you, I knew I had made one enormous blunder - once was simply not enough." He dropped a tender kiss on her temple, pulled her closer into his side and chuckled. "I've spent the better part of the day plotting and planning ways to meet you again," he nodded to someone as they made their way down the escalator to the lush green lawns, trackside. "In fact," he continued, "my staff are ready to kick me. I have been so distracted all day, thinking about you and last night, when I should be focusing on my job of training horses, on a race day that is crucial for my stables." They continued to weave their way through the steadily building crowds, as Michael continued. "Can you imagine the thrill I felt when walking towards the suite, to meet up with Nana, and I saw you standing at the window sipping champagne?"

"So much for trying to get away," Jane muttered

Michael crowed with laughter. "I saw you dart away when I arrived, and then you went straight to my Nana, I very nearly yelled 'Eureka' right there in the poshest suite at Randwick."

They looked at each and laughed. "Well I would have liked to have seen some of the reactions to that."

"Nah they're used to me and my enthusiasm, though I have to say, it would be the first time I had ever called 'Eureka' for a woman." He shot her a playful smile. "I usually reserve that for my winning horses."

"Well thank you! I'm delighted a rank up there with a winner."

"Oh, Jane you are such a winner," Michael leaned down and kissed her hungrily. They quickly pulled apart when a cheeky whistle pierced their erotic bubble. Jane resisted the urge to fan herself after that scorching hot kiss as they continued to navigate their way through the crowds.

"Hey, boss, over here."

Michael swerved towards the man who had attracted his

attention, quickly making his way to him where he stood with a beautiful chestnut horse, which had a prominent white forelock and eyes that were alert and eager. Michael stopped and whispered to the horse, all the while holding Jane close.

"Would you be the person that was responsible for my boss being late for morning gallops for the first time ever?"

"No comment," responded Jane with a sly smile.

"Hi, I'm Stacey," the man introduced himself with a knowing smile. "Mike has been incredibly distracted this morning, however with you tucked up next to him I'm seeing a vast improvement in his concentration, thank goodness!"

Ah, so this is Stacey of the early morning phone call. Obviously not a lover but a colleague and a male one at that.

Laughter bubbled inside her and jealousy receded as she responded with an outstretched hand and a broad smile. "Jane Bryce, lovely to meet you."

"Leave off with the commentary Stacey," commented Mike as he entered the conversation, "Sometimes Stacey can be too cheeky." He flashed a smile at Jane and sent Stacey off on an errand, leaving them alone. "Jane come and meet Tiger's Eye, or Tigs, as we like to call him."

Jane stepped up and stroked the beautiful animal. Due to her dad's involvement with owning horses, she was incredibly comfortable around them.

Michael leaned in close. "Tigs was the last colt my grandpa purchased before his death, and he insisted on it being named Tiger's Eye for my Nana."

She looked up at this tall man who towered over her not so petite frame. "Homage to Barbara's love for the stone."

Shaking his head, "Not so much - when my grandparents became engaged, Pa was broke, and they chose an engagement ring at Paddy's Market." Jane watched as a softness wash over his face. "My Nana fell in love with the tiger's eye ring, and no matter how many times Pa offered to buy her a new ring over the years, Nana refused to relinquish that engagement ring, and wore it every day. My grandpa always said it was the ultimate act of love and respect for their marriage that she insisted on keeping that simple ring. This horse, and the name, was his final act of love for my Nana."

Jane could see his throat moving as he held his feelings in check and she felt the tightening in her chest as emotion threatened to swamp her composure.

"Can you see, Jane, that I'm a good bet for a second date." He spoke softly to her and continued. "I get why you're hesitant about relationships with a serial divorcee like your dad, but my family history will counterbalance your crazy family history."

"My crazy family history, that's harsh, true but harsh. What about your parents - are they still married?" she teased.

"Well if you were to take up my offer of a second date, you could be my plus one at their 40th-wedding anniversary, which is next week. I know that our second date will be terrific, so it could be a fourth or fifth date."

A laugh exploded from Jane. "Four or five dates in one week? I don't think so."

With that, he placed a soft, almost reverent, kiss on her mouth "Then please let's take a chance and start with one date... tonight?"

Jane was stunned that he would make so much effort to woo a reluctant woman in a public place with such a large crowd swirling around them. If Michael could be this brave, well hell, so could she! Reaching up, she wrapped her arms around his neck and softly played with the curls sitting on that crisp white collar. Michael held perfectly still while he waited for her answer, his body radiating that energy which had drawn her to him last night.

"OK, dinner tonight, and let us see if we're not done."

2

WANDERER

HOLLEE MANDS

Wintry air caressed with errant fingers, drawing prickles on her skin. Qaia shivered, tightening the kaftan around her shoulders as she gazed at the river meandering through tall pines and silver ferns. Seated cross-legged on the forest floor, she waited. As soon as the last leaf fell, she would be forced to leave the village. Like all wanderers, Qaia detested the cold, and her mule-skin tent couldn't withstand the frost. But now, even the promise of warmer climes no longer appealed.

A tiny, warm bundle clambered out of her pocket to perch on her shoulder. Qaia grinned and held out an open palm. Tiger scurried on without hesitation, peering at her with a single, inquisitive eye the colour of darkest midnight.

"You miss him, huh?" She stroked the sugar glider's velvety pelt with a forefinger. A pink nose twitched in response. "Me too," she sighed.

A shadow loomed on her periphery.

Pulse skipping like a pebble over a placid lake, Qaia set Tiger to the ground before jumping to her feet to embrace familiar warmth.

"Who misses me?" drawled a deep timbred voice — sensual and soothing. Ensconced in the scent of warm leather and spice, Qaia traced the strong lines of his jaw. "Tiger," she declared with mock nonchalance. "And only because you bear treats."

He chuckled, eyes gleaming like the ocean on a clear summer's day. "Hmm, is that so?" he murmured before tipping her chin to claim her lips.

Time seemed to still. The chill of the winds tamed amidst the tangle of tongues and roving limbs. When they finally broke apart — flushed and breathless —Axel lowered himself to the mossy embankment. Drawing her onto his lap, he reached into his leather satchel to produce a handful of berries. Tiger scampered closer, eyeing the proffered treat with great interest. Axel clucked his tongue. The sugar glider emitted a high-pitched chatter, then clambered onto his callused hand to gorge. Qaia couldn't help the quirk of her lips. Axel had charmed even her shy and wary companion.

"I've certainly missed *you*." He pressed soft kisses against the side of her temple, husky words fanning embers of hope in her heart. Had their clandestine meetings become more than a lover's tryst for him too? Would he miss her when she left?

"There has been another attack," he said.

Her throat tightened. "Where?"

"A farm up north." Axel firmed his jaw. "The beast managed to slip away before my men and I arrived. The farmer — what was left of him— was found strewn over the field."

A shudder trailed down her spine. The last 'victim' had been discovered in the outskirts of the village. Savaged so badly, the body had been unidentifiable.

"Will you keep hunting?" Qaia asked, even though she already knew his answer.

"It is a huntsman's duty to keep his village safe." His voice was quiet, but his tone resolute. Disappointment tunnelled through her. Axel would never leave the village or forsake his duty. And a wanderer had no place in a society that would shun and sunder their relationship.

Qaia unfastened the leather strap around her neck, drawing out an amulet fashioned from a stone sacred to her people. The Tiger's Eye gleamed in the moonlight, slivers of gold glinting through the russet stone.

"I want you to have this," she said.

Axel's brows furrowed. "I can't, it belonged to your mother." The only heirloom Qaia had, it was beyond precious. But Axel was her heart.

"This has protected me for all the years I've wandered. Now I hope it will protect you." She could not bear the vision of Axel falling prey to the fangs and claws of the encroaching beast with a taste for human flesh.

Axel's large hands closed over hers, covering the amulet in her grasp. "Then I shall wear it with pride and honour. For after this hunt, I will protect you for the rest of my days."

Qaia blinked, lips parting at the significance of his words. This, she had not foreseen. "I cannot bear the thought of life without you, sweet Qaia," he murmured, causing her pulse to escalate like rapids before a fall.

"But your village will never accept a pairing between a huntsman and a wanderer," she protested. He met her gaze with unflinching eyes that promised a lifetime of love and happiness.

"Once this threat is eradicated, we'll leave the village. You've always longed for the ocean, have you not? We'll travel south, to one of the smaller, coastal towns and make a quiet life. Just the two of us." The lump on his throat bobbed, and he gave a nervous laugh. "Just the three of us," he amended, giving the now sluggish sugar glider a reconciliatory pat before fishing something small from his pocket.

A gold ring.

"Will you marry me, Qaia?"

CXXO

Qaia tightened her cloak, keeping the hood over her head and her gaze lowered. With her dark hair and unusual eyes, it was impossible to hide her wanderer's blood, hence she rarely ventured into the village. Yet, with her heart fluttering like a windswept dandelion, Qaia felt eager for a stroll in the sunshine. Never had she envisioned a home and hearth. Or a husband who could make her breath hitch with a single smouldering gaze. Qaia bit her lower lip to stymie the smile that lingered long after Axel had left her tent the previous night.

"Now, keep out of sight if you want some honey cake," she

said to the glider riding the lapels of her cloak. Tiger blinked a singular eye, chattering his annoyance as she tucked him into the folds of her pocket. Like her, Tiger was a peculiar creature. Perhaps it was their peculiarity that drew them together — two half-blind creatures.

"I'm sorry but I don't think the baker appreciates marsupials in his shop," she whispered. Or wanderers for that matter, but she had a yen to celebrate the golden band around her finger with something sweet.

"Three pieces of silver," droned the balding shopkeeper, decorated from head to toe with patches of stray flour. Another patron bustled by, knocking the silver out of Qaia's hands.

"Oh dear, clumsy me," The woman ran a hand over her protruding belly, "I'm sorry, these days, I can't even see my own toes..."

The pregnant woman looked up and their gazes collided. Her sharp intake of breath caused Qaia's heart to quicken like a rabbit under a fox's scrutiny. The woman curved her arms around her belly — as if to shield her unborn child from Qaia's proximity.

Spine rigid, Qaia snatched up the wrapped honey cakes and deposited the silver into the hands of the now curious stallholder. He peered beneath her hood, and his lips curled as though he viewed a gutter rat. "Get out," he spat. "Don't need no *wanderer* contaminating my shop."

Pinning him with a steely eyed glare, Qaia had the satisfaction of seeing him flinch. "It's the likes of you that led the beast to our village," he growled.

Qaia could understand society's fear of wanderers. She'd even come to accept it. Most feared what they could not understand, but their ignorance grated her like sandpaper. "We may be gifted with the sight, but we are *not* harbingers of bad luck," she snapped.

"Just leave us, please," the pregnant woman shuddered,

eyes carefully averted as if the mere sight of her would bestow calamity.

Qaia stifled her retort and marched toward the exit.

"To think that creature bested *all* our huntsmen…" The softly spoken lament caused Qaia to pause mid step.

"A bloodbath," grunted the shopkeeper. "Never heard of such an intelligent beast. Evaded capture by throwing some men over the edge of the cliff, it did."

Qaia stiffened, blood coagulating to ice. "Did any of the huntsmen survive?"

The shopkeeper scowled, folding his brawny arms. "Didn't I tell you to get out?"

"The huntsmen," Qaia repeated through clenched teeth, heart tightening into a painful vice. "Did any of them survive?"

"There were *no* survivors."

∞∞∞

Qaia dug her toes into the warm sand, drawing a deep breath of the briny breeze. She shut her eyes, allowing the gentle percussion of waves and the distant caw of gulls to lull her into a false state of peace. Tiger, as if sensing her emotions, darted out of her pocket to clamber up her forearm.

"I miss him too," she whispered. Tiger curled into the crook of her neck, a smidgen of warmth that did nothing to dull the permanent ache in her chest.

Two years, and still she mourned him every day.

Longed for him every night.

She'd made a life by the coastal town her huntsman had once promised her forever. Trying to piece together the shattered remains of her heart. Yet, each day she would gaze into the shimmering expanse of turquoise — the very shade of Axel's eyes — and sadness would seep into her veins.

"I miss you so much," she whispered into the caressing breeze and capering waves.

When the tears finally ebbed, Qaia strolled down the dunes, toward the dock. Boats dotted the distance, bobbing in the sea. Fishermen drew in their catch, sailors milled, and tradesmen unloaded wares from large ships. As she drew close, there were no discerning remarks or judgemental eyes. People barely paid her any attention in this little port, bustling with activity. They were too busy going about their lives to notice her bicoloured eyes.

A silhouette in the distance drew her attention.

The man strolled the dock with a steady gait that was achingly familiar. Tall and lean, with broad shoulders she knew with intimate knowledge. It was too far to make out his visage, but his profile bore the same chiselled lines that haunted her dreams. Her mouth went dry, pulse churning like waves in a maelstrom.

"Watch out!"

Qaia collided headfirst into a man with weathered-brown skin, carting a barrel of fish. "Ye ought to watch where yer' goin, girlie," grumbled the man as he righted the upended barrel.

"Sorry," Qaia mumbled as her eyes scoured the docks for the vision that had led to her collision. The silhouette was gone.

Simply a hallucination borne of the terrible yearning of her heart.

જ્જ

Axel strolled past pedlars shouting wares and cajoling shopkeepers. Meandering through the streets, he took care to move out of the way of delivery wagons and handcarts trundling over cobbled walkways. He'd spent the entire day at sea, working the nets, and was in sore need of a pint. Instead of walking into the local tavern, Axel's feet invariably turned down the main street lined with traders, toward the lone merchant selling handwoven baskets.

She always wore a dark cloak that shrouded most of her appearance, but Axel had been riveted by her voice. Captivated by the gentle grace of her mannerisms. He hadn't felt this drawn to anything since the day he'd woken from the stupor that had stolen most of his memories.

He ambled closer, itching to strike up conversation. Yet the gold band glinting on her finger held him back. No decent man should harbour such yearning for a married woman. He indulged himself by watching her from a distance, soaking in the soft bell of her voice and the delicate curve of her lips as she made another sale. She kept her head lowered. The hood made it impossible to see her eyes, and the cloak covered most of her physique — but it did nothing to dampen the urge in his heart. The same urge that had propelled him to leave his village and led him to this tiny, coastal town. He had no idea what he was doing here, only that it felt *right*. When he'd first laid eyes on the merchant, the same chord of rightness had struck him hard in the chest.

Sighing, Axel had turned to leave when he caught sight of a young boy lurking at the sidelines. The boy sidled close to the unsuspecting merchant, nimble fingers reaching out for the merchant's satchel.

"Stop, thief!" Axel shouted, startling the boy. The merchant snapped her head up in surprise, but the boy was already twisting through the crowds like a slippery eel, prize in hand.

Axel gave chase.

The thief sped by a vegetable stall and sent a basket of fruit tumbling in his wake. Axel sailed past orange missiles and an enraged stallholder, determined not to lose his quarry. As the pickpocket turned down a less crowded street, Axel seized him by the collar — the boy might be adroit at skirting stalls and dodging crowds, but Axel had far longer legs.

"Lemme go, you cur!" cried the wriggling bandit.

"You little scapegrace, return the lady's satchel," he said. Lips forming a grim line, the boy reluctantly relinquished the pouch. Judging from the boy's unkempt hair and tattered garb, he was a street urchin. Axel drew out a coin from his own pocket and handed it to the child. "If you need a job, look for me at the docks on the 'morrow," he said, "but don't let me catch you stealing again." Once released, the boy blinked his relief and darted off quicker than a mouse in a corn field.

Lighter footsteps approached from behind. The merchant woman slowed to a jog, panting to regain her breath. She flipped up her hood to reveal hair as dark as midnight and creamy skin that made his fingers itch. When their gazes locked, the air was knocked right out of his lungs. The most extraordinary pair of eyes stared back at him — one iris was filmed over with a cloudy grey that indicated sightlessness. But the other was a startling shade of amber rimmed with black.

A wanderer.

Only those blessed with the sight bore such distinctive eyes. And she was the most beautiful woman he'd ever seen.

She was staring at him as though he was a ghost. Her lips parted, but no words escaped. Axel swallowed, trying to dispel the riotous sense of recognition in his chest. Did they know each other? His hand trailed inadvertently under his shirt to grasp the amulet he'd never taken off.

"Axel?" Her voice was a whisper filled with raw emotion.

He blinked. She *knew* his name? "Should I know you, miss?"

Tears filled her eyes.

Axel swallowed. Clearly, she *knew* him. She was small, and standing close, he realised she barely reached his chin. He dipped his head to study her face, cursing his lost memories. Who was she?

"Is it really you, Axel?" She began sobbing in earnest, disbelief in every word.

"Yes. What's your name?" he asked, desperate to unravel the mystery.

"Qaia," she said through tears. "My name is Qaia."

He bridged the distance between them, hands moving on their own volition to catch a stray tear with his thumb. The movement seemed to unravel her. With a loud sob, she threw her arms around his neck, burying her face into his chest. Startled by her forwardness, Axel stiffened. Yet, she felt *right* in his arms.

"Qaia," he murmured, her name rolling off his tongue like the smoothest honey. She even smelled familiar, like vanilla tinged with a subtle fragrance that was uniquely her.

"How can this be?" Gentle hands reached up to cup his cheeks. "I thought you to be dead."

Axel swallowed again. "You must forgive me. I lost my memories two years ago. A beast sent me hurtling down a cliff," he tapped the faint scar at the side of his temple, "and I woke to discover I've forgotten most of everything."

Her eyes widened. "But how did you know where to find me?"

Axel clapped his hand to his chest. "This amulet," he breathed, drawing out the stone from beneath his tunic. "Led me here." *To you*, he wanted to say, but her ring glinted, and he held his tongue. She grasped the amulet, her vivid eye glinting with a myriad of emotion. With a jolt, he realised her seeing eye was the very colour of the amulet in his possession.

A Tiger's Eye.

"I was in your village three years ago where I first met my fiancé."

Axel's heart plummeted.

"I gave this to him, to keep him safe." She trailed her fingers over the amulet and a placed a hand over his chest in a gesture that was both intimate and familiar. "Wanderers also believe the Tiger's Eye acts as a guiding star in times of turbulence."

His lips parted, and their gazes locked. Time seemed to still, the cacophony of the market melting to the background. His lips curved as understanding converged with recognition.

"It led me back to you," he murmured, leaning forward, compelled to taste her lips.

She tilted up her head, rising to the tip of her toes to meet him halfway. A furry creature darted abruptly from the folds of her cloak to peer at him with one large eye, thwarting the moment. Startled, Axel jerked back.

Her laughter was vibrant, like the tinkle of windchimes. "Tiger is simply curious."

"Tiger..." He studied the one-eyed sugar glider sniffing at his outstretched fingers. A glimmer of memory danced at the edges of his mind. "And has Tiger missed me?"

Her smile, as bright as her laughter, filled the part in his heart he'd always known was missing. "So very much," she whispered, before their lips met.

3

CLARITY

LISA STANBRIDGE

I *can do this.*

Standing at the end of the hallway, Hannah stared out the open front door. She twisted her hands together, breathing in slowly through her nose and out through her mouth. It was simple. All she had to do was step through it, get into her car and drive to work.

A warm afternoon spring breeze wafted inside. She closed her eyes, letting it caress her skin, catch on her hair, and calm her racing heart. Breathing in deeply, she caught the scent of roses and smiled. Yes, she *could* do this.

It'd been a month since she'd been assaulted and mugged in the park. The police had labelled it a random attack, a druggie desperate for money. He'd been caught and jailed, Hannah was safe, but anxiety still controlled her life. For the first two weeks she couldn't even step outside. She could now, *just*, but the fear was crippling.

"Are you okay?"

She spun around at the voice, her heart warming at the sight of her best friend and housemate, Liam. He'd been a godsend over the last month, never letting her deal with this alone, and helping her face the world again.

Pulling her shoulders back, she forced a smile. "I'm fine."

He raised his eyebrows and stepped forward. Stopping in front of her, Liam's gaze met hers, his grey-blue eyes questioning. "Are you sure?"

Her heart slammed against her chest. Emotion overwhelmed her, a lump forming in her throat. Who was she fooling? Of course she wasn't fine, but she couldn't stay in hiding forever.

Tears pooled beneath her eyelids and she shook her head. "Okay, maybe not." She gave him a watery smile. "But I will be. My sick leave has officially run out, so I need to return to work."

Liam smiled and held out his arms. She accepted his embrace, snuggling into the warmth of his hard chest.

He tightened his hold around her, securing her in a safe cocoon she never wanted to leave. "I'm proud of you, Hannah."

She smiled and inhaled deeply, never wanting to forget his masculine scent tinged with exotic spice. Had she mentioned she was head over heels in love with him?

He'd made it clear they'd only ever be friends, but that'd never stopped her feelings from growing stronger with each passing day.

"Why spoil a good thing?" That was the question he'd asked when she'd confessed to having a crush on him in high school. It was the single most awkward moment of her life.

It'd nearly ended their friendship, taking them months to get back to normal. Now, terrified of repeating this and losing him completely, she suffered in silence. Being housemates was better than nothing, right?

Liam let her go and she reluctantly stepped away.

"Oh," he patted his pockets, but when he didn't find what he was looking for, he held up a finger and said, "hold on a sec, I have something for you."

He dashed to his room and reappeared seconds later with a thin rectangular box. He held it out and placed it in her hand. Hannah gasped as she opened the lid and removed a shining golden necklace. Its elegant teardrop pendant glinted in the afternoon sunlight, glowing a warm yellow-gold, with streaks of brown through it.

"Liam," she breathed, "it's beautiful."

He held out his hand for the necklace. "May I?"

She nodded and passed it to him. Turning, she pulled her light brown curls over her shoulder. Liam lowered the necklace over her head and clasped it in place. Her heart raced when his fingers grazed her skin, leaving fire in their wake. She bit her lip, a shiver rippling down her spine, right to her toes. She spun around, her gaze clashing with his. A spark of excitement followed the shiver through her body. There was no hiding the want and need in the gaze he returned. He *did* have feelings for her! When had it changed?

Liam blinked as though waking from a dream and took a step back, lowering his eyes. Her brow furrowed. Why was he pushing her away?

She looked down at the pendant to hide her disappointment, running her thumb over the smooth, cool stone.

"The gem is a tiger's eye," Liam explained. "It's apparently supposed to help with clarity of mind, and coping with fear and anxiety. I thought, after everything you've been through, it might help."

She glanced up at him and smiled, touched by his gesture. "Thank you." She placed her arms around his neck and embraced him.

When he pulled away, she kept her arms secured around him. She met his gaze once more and sent him a silent message.

Kiss me. Please. This doesn't have to ruin anything.

His eyes flicked to her lips and his pupils dilated. He wanted it as much as she did, there was no mistaking it. Their faces were so close, their breath mixed. Just a couple of inches closer and they'd kiss. Boldness overcame her. She moved towards him, her lips only millimetres away from his. He closed the distance, their lips brushing. It was barely a whisper, but it sent her heart racing, bolts of electricity reaching every nerve ending in her body.

Suddenly there was cold space between them as Liam stumbled back, his face contorting in shock. Confused, she shook her head and opened her mouth a couple of times to speak, but she couldn't form any words.

"Hannah—" Liam ran his hands down his face and sighed heavily. "I'm sorry, that shouldn't have happened."

"Why?" she blurted. "We're not in high school anymore. This isn't just a crush, Liam."

Liam paced back and forth in the hallway. "It's got nothing to do with high school."

"Then what is it?" She raised her hands in question.

He stopped pacing and turned to her, contrite. His forehead was crinkled, frustration etched in the lines of his face. He opened his mouth to speak but instead he shook his head and strode away.

Rejected by Liam. Again. Her face flamed, humiliation and embarrassment overwhelming the crippling fear of stepping outside. Now she was desperate to get out. With an angry sigh, Hannah turned and left for her evening shift at work.

৩৪৪৩

"Can I speak to you for a moment?"

Hannah looked up from the book she was reading on the

sofa. Liam stood in front of the TV, hands stuffed in his jeans pocket. She nodded and closed her book, putting it aside. Having a whole day to think about what'd happened, she was more confused than ever. She couldn't deny him the opportunity to explain when she was desperate for answers.

"I'm sorry about yesterday," Liam said, his eyes reflecting his genuine apology.

She swallowed and sat forward. "I'm sorry too. If I made you uncomfortable or—"

"No, you didn't." Liam sat beside her, knotting his hands in his lap. He was silent for a long moment before he looked at her, determination in his eyes. "I care about you, Hannah. Probably more than I should."

What did that mean? Her eyebrows drew together, but she didn't speak.

"In fact," he lowered his gaze, "I think I've loved you ever since you told me you had a crush on me, if not before."

Her heart leapt. It took every ounce of willpower not to break out into a silly grin and do a happy jig around the lounge room. It was only suspecting there was more to come that stopped her.

"Why didn't you say anything?" she whispered.

He shrugged and stood again, pacing the floor in front of the sofa. "I felt like I botched everything up, so I wanted to let some time pass. When you started dating other people, I knew I had to move on too, so I did the same thing. Whenever we were both single at the same time, I tried to find the courage to tell you the truth, but the timing was always wrong. Then—" He raised his eyes heavenward and blew out a long breath.

Dread settled in the pit of her stomach like an iron ball. "Then what?"

He stopped and stood in front of her, keeping his head bowed. "Do you remember my last girlfriend, Carla?"

"Yes, I remember."

She was the last girl he'd dated. Their relationship had ended a year ago.

He finally lifted his head and looked at her. His eyes were dark and sorrowful. "When we started dating, she asked me to have a fertility test." His cheeks reddened. "She made it clear that she only dated with the view of having a family. I didn't see the harm in it, after all, if we didn't last, which we didn't, I figured it'd be good to know for the future."

Hannah froze and her heart stilled. She managed a nod. She was sure her face had turned pale, if the cold sweat washing over her was anything to go by.

Liam sighed heavily and in one breath said, "I'm infertile."

And there it was. The bombshell. The words hit her like daggers, right to the chest. The air was knocked out of her. No explanation needed. Those two words explained everything.

"Wow," was all she could say. "I wasn't expecting that."

Liam's crestfallen face made her heart crumble into tiny pieces. Family was everything to him, *and* her.

"Liam, I'm so sorry. That's... that's—" she shook her head, words failing her.

In the past they'd often talked about how their kids would grow up together. Although she'd always secretly dreamed of having children *together*.

Now it wasn't a possibility. Was their relationship doomed before it even began, because of this massive barrier?

Standing on trembling legs, she paced the floor, her hands clenching and unclenching at her sides.

"Hannah," Liam appeared in front of her, taking her hands, "I'm sorry. I'd do anything to be with you, but how can I deprive you of the privilege of having children? Hell, it kills me to do this but I'm trying to be fair on you."

She ripped her hands away. "Fair? How's it fair when you've already made up your mind? If you really wanted us to have a future, shouldn't we have discussed it together?"

He winced. "Alright, that was wrong of me. I'm sorry. But you can't deny it changes things. I can see it in your eyes, Hannah, you're questioning if it can still work."

She lowered her eyes, hating that he saw right through her. Was there any way they could overlook it? Could they commit to never having children together?

Her head spun. There was so much to think about.

"Liam, I—" she furrowed her brow, unsure what she was supposed to say. Instead she said, "I need to think about this," then turned and disappeared into her bedroom.

ഗ്രാജ

It'd been a week since Liam's confession. Hannah had been rostered night shifts for the week and, with Liam working during the day, they barely saw each other. They went about their lives like nothing was different.

But everything *was* different, and she still hadn't processed everything.

When she'd finished the nightly medication run and her patients were sleeping, she took a break. She went into a bathroom and splashed cold water over her face. After patting it dry, she stared at her reflection in the mirror. Bags had formed under her eyes, the night shifts taking their toll. Thankfully this was her last one for a week.

Her gaze landed on the pendant hanging around her neck, which she wore daily. Did it really help the way Liam had said it would? Strangely, her anxiety levels had reduced significantly, but couldn't that just be because she was back in routine?

There was only one way to find out.

Grasping the pendant, she squeezed her eyes shut and thought of Liam. What she loved about him and how they complemented each other. Living together was so natural. They'd been sharing a house for five years as friends and they'd been the happiest years of her life. Wasn't the most important thing in a relationship about being happy together?

An image of his face came into her mind, his grey-blue eyes shining brightly as they stared at her with love. Her eyes flew open and she let go of the pendant. It fell against her skin and calmness came over her, along with clarity of mind.

She knew exactly what she wanted to do.

ය෴ාද

Hannah entered the house the next afternoon after going for a walk with a friend. She'd made a new resolution to leave the house once a day, even when she wasn't working.

After closing the door, she turned, just as Liam came out of his room, dressed to go out. "Are you going somewhere?" she asked.

"I'm meeting a potential client to discuss their wedding photos," Liam replied.

Hannah nodded and went into her room to change. She stopped in front of her built-in wardrobe, sliding the doors open, and flicked through the dresses, deciding what to wear.

"You're heading out too?" Liam asked.

She glanced over her shoulder to find him standing in her doorway. "I need to do some shopping." She inspected a dress with a wrinkle of her nose.

"I think you should wear this one." Liam appeared behind her and reached in for one, pressing his chest against her back.

Her body sparked to life and her eyes fluttered closed, relishing his closeness. She released a shuddering breath and turned. Now chest to chest with him, she slowly lifted her gaze to meet his. He looked at her with such intensity, such *love*.

Liam cleared his throat and stepped back, holding out the dress.

"Thanks." She took it from him and held it out to inspect. It was a white summer dress that came to her knees in an A-line, decorated with embroidered flowers.

She grinned. "Good choice, I haven't worn this for ages."

"You always look beautiful in it."

Her cheeks flushed. She smiled at him before laying the dress on her bed. Turning back to her closet, she removed a pair of sandals.

"Hannah?"

Placing the shoes on the floor next to her bed, she spun around to find Liam hovering at her door, preparing to leave. "Yeah?"

He stared at her for a long moment. His eyes were pleading, asking her to put him out of his misery. In the end he sighed and, in a resigned voice, said, "I'd better go. Have a good afternoon."

"You too."

When the front door closed a few seconds later, she sat on the edge of her bed, guilt eating away at her. Breathing in deeply, she held it for a second then released it slowly. She hadn't meant to make him wait. Even though she knew what she wanted, finding the right words was hard. Sometime today she *would* talk to him.

Half an hour later she left. On the way to the shopping centre, she passed a quaint little park. When she spotted Liam's car parked nearby, she gasped. It had to be a sign! Once she'd pulled into the next vacant parking space, she went in search of Liam. She found him at the rotunda, still with his client. She obscured herself in the background behind a tree and waited for them to finish.

It was about ten minutes later when they shook hands and went their separate ways. Hannah drew in a deep breath. *This is it.* She touched the pendant as though for strength, then approached him. Birds chirped in the trees above, laughter sounded from the playground nearby, and the warm spring sun beat down on her.

When Liam spotted her, he stumbled to a stop. "Hannah? What are you doing here? How'd you know I'd be here?"

"I spotted your car." She wiped her sweaty palms along the skirt of her dress. "I, uh, wanted to talk to you."

He came closer and stopped in front of her, his eyes searching hers. "Oh?"

She nodded and swallowed hard. "I'm really sorry I left the way I did last week, and I'm sorry it took me so long to figure myself out." She drew in another breath. "I love you, Liam. If you want to be with me, I want us to give this a shot."

Liam's eyes shimmered with tears, a wide smile stretching across his face. He took her hands. "Hannah, I want nothing more than to be with you, but what about—"

She shook her head and squeezed his hands. "I think this should be about us right now. We're not going in blind. If this is real between us, and we decide to start a family, we'll explore other options like treatments for fertility issues, or even adoption. But right now, why should it stop us from being together? From loving each other?"

Liam stared at her for a long moment, his eyes wide and glistening. When a lone tear dripped down his cheek, he cursed and wiped it away, his face turning red. "Geez, woman, what are you doing to me?"

She laughed and stood on tiptoes to kiss his cheek. "I'm in for the long haul, if that's what you want."

Liam released one of her hands and stroked her cheek,

staring at her intently. "Are you sure?"

"I've never been surer of anything in my life."

"Oh, Hannah," he rested his forehead against hers, "I can't tell you how much that means to me. I love you. Of course I want to make this work."

With clarity came the ability to make wise and *right* decisions. So, when Liam kissed her, *finally*, it was perfect, without hesitation, and everything she'd imagined it would be. The softness of his lips, the gentleness of the kiss, and the promise of what was to come only strengthened her confidence that they were always meant to be.

4

THE FLIGHT

SUE-ELLEN PASHLEY

"**G**od. Oh God. It's so small!"

Beside me, Sam sighed and reached into her bag.

"You'll be fine," she said, straightening back up, having found what she was looking for straight away. Of course. Her handbag was meticulous, everything exactly where it was supposed to be. I shoved mine further under the seat with my foot. No need for comparisons. "It's the same plane you flew here on and you obviously survived that."

"Yes, but statistically, that probably makes it worse."

"No," she said, flicking her hair over her shoulder. "It doesn't. That's not how it works. Anyway, I have something for you. Something to help. Give me your wrist."

I held out my hand like the dutiful, younger sister I was, and she fastened a bracelet around it. The round stones were cool against my skin and I touched them with my finger. They were deep brown with swirls and flecks of gold and amber.

"Pretty."

She nodded. "Tiger's eye. They're a protection stone, especially when travelling. They're supposed to attract good luck as well. And help with organisation." Her eyes flicked down to my bag and I shoved it again.

"Do you think it'll help?" I twisted it around my wrist, stomach still knotting as I looked out the window to the plane again.

"Imogen Celeste Brown, you are not going to die on that plane. It's perfectly safe."

I groaned. "Don't say the D word. It makes it worse."

She sighed again. Those sighs were really starting to bug me.

"Let's people watch then," she said. "It'll take your mind off it. Mmm, check out the guy over there in the suit."

I wrinkled my nose at her choice. We had different taste in men. In fact, we had different taste in most things. And we looked nothing alike. Sam was tall with blonde hair and an ample chest, whereas I was dark, short and flat. Petite, Mum used to say, like that made it better. The guy she'd pointed out had blond hair, cut aggressively in an almost-crewcut, and was dressed in a sharp, grey suit. I could feel the alpha male pheromones from here.

"Definitely not my type." My eyes searched the small airport. "Over there. He's much better."

He was tall with dark hair and a three-day growth that had just a hint of roughness. Blue shirt that highlighted a nice chest and arms. Yummy.

Sam snorted. "It's a shame about the wife and kid."

"Shut up. Don't wreck my fantasy. It's not like anything's going to happen. I can imagine."

"That's your problem. You're always imagining, never doing."

It was my turn to sigh. I could feel this heading to another lecture about the sad state of my love life. I watched the guy with his family instead, tuning out her voice. His arm was wrapped around the woman and they laughed as the little girl acted out something in front of them. She was dressed in a rainbow of colours; a pink, glittery cowboy hat finishing the ensemble. A kid with pizzazz. I liked her. And then the guy swooped her into a hug, lifting her up and tickling her. Their joy was infectious and I smiled, even though my chest hurt a little watching them. That right there. That's what I wanted.

"Flight 713 to Brisbane is now boarding at Gate 3."

I gripped Sam's hand. "Oh God."

She squeezed my hand back. "You've got the tiger's eye, remember? You'll be fine."

I nodded, mouth dry. Right. The tiger's eye. I just needed to focus on that. But the plane seemed even smaller out on the tarmac and I could feel the panic building in my chest, spreading, like it was systematically taking over every cell in my body. I twisted the bracelet, feeling the coolness of the stones, trying to remember to breathe.

ᘓᘔ

Stuffing my bag under the seat, I fastened my belt with shaky hands, focusing on my breathing. In and out. In and out. It was only just keeping the panic at bay, and we weren't even off the ground yet.

I looked at the people filing down the aisle instead, trying to keep my mind from going down dark paths. The guy in blue was waiting patiently as a woman tried to shove an obviously-too-big bag into the overhead locker. She must have asked for help because he pushed it in for her and she smiled at him. A flash of jealousy speared through me. Stupid.

And then he was continuing down the aisle, closer, closer until he stopped next to me, putting his bag in the locker. He smiled as he sat down, blue eyes wrinkling at the corners. A dark blue I could easily lose myself in. And damn, he smelt good. A slight whiff of cologne but something else as well. Earthy. Nice.

Nice with wife and child that he's just left in the airport. Get a grip!

CʒꙄꙂ

By some great twist of fate, I was sitting next to the woman I'd noticed in the airport. Honestly, she'd been hard to miss. Dark long hair, brown eyes that, up this close, had flecks of gold. Tiny, but there was a strength in the way she moved. I think that's what made me keep looking over at her. Brave enough to get on a plane when it obviously freaked the hell out of her, if the nervous breathing as the staff went through the safety procedures was anything to go by.

I watched her out of the corner of my eye as we left the ground. She gave a soft moan and I wondered if she was actually going to throw up. And whether I should offer her the bag out of my seat pocket or if that'd make it worse. She was gripping the armrests so hard her fingers were turning white, but then let go to twist the bracelet she was wearing instead. Round and round.

I gave her a sympathetic smile. "Not a fan of flying?"

She grimaced. "Not really. And the statistics and facts don't help."

ஐ

He laughed. Dear God, even his laugh was perfect, like it was on the same frequency as my ovaries.

"No, they usually don't. When your stress response kicks in, it's hard to persuade it that you're okay when you're still on the plane."

I nodded at him. "Right! Most people don't understand that. Everyone keeps lecturing me about how safe flying is, blah, blah, blah. Like I'm stupid and I don't know that already."

"Is the bracelet a good luck charm?"

I realised I was still twisting it like some sort of maniac.

"Sort of. My sister gave it to me at the airport. It's tiger's eye. Apparently it protects you when you're travelling and brings good luck. And something else too. Organisation maybe?"

He smiled. My heart did a quick step and it wasn't because of fear this time.

"Is organisation something you need help with?"

I felt the heat on my cheeks and he laughed again.

"I'll take the blush as a yes."

Laughing with him, I realised I hadn't thought about panicking for at least a minute. It was a miracle.

"I'm Chris." He turned slightly in his seat, hand out, and I shook it. It engulfed mine and I wondered what it'd feel like on my body, running down the side of my waist, cupping my –

God, stop it! He obviously wasn't available!

"Imogen," I said, withdrawing my hand.

ෲ

Christ, I hadn't been this nervous since high school. I pushed my hand through my hair, not knowing what to do with it. Wishing she hadn't let go. She wasn't wearing a ring but that didn't mean she wasn't in a relationship. God, I really hoped she wasn't.

"And are you heading to Brisbane for business or pleasure?"

Please be business. Please be business.

She screwed up her nose in a way that made me want to kiss her. Right then and there.

"I'm heading home, but going back to work, so I guess a bit of both. But home is Sydney, not Brisbane."

My heart sat up and took notice, like a bear scenting something on the wind. I tried to act cool though. Unaffected.

"I'm heading to Sydney too. My flight's not 'til this afternoon though. 3.10, I think."

She smiled, one that made it to her eyes. "We'll be on the same flight." And then the smile faltered and I wondered what she was thinking. It was frustrating that I didn't have a clue. "What about you? Are you flying for business?"

"No. Going home too. My sister's a single mum and had to go in for an operation so I've been looking after my niece while she recovered. It'll be nice to get back to my own place though. And the quiet!"

The smile was back, bigger this time, and I wanted to take her in my arms and protect her and make sure she always smiled like that. Neanderthal man stuff. Which was... different. For me, anyway. And slightly unsettling.

"Was that them at the airport? The little girl in the pink hat you hugged?"

"That's her. Billie." I narrowed my eyes at her, trying not to smile like an idiot. "You noticed me then?"

The heat was back in her cheeks. "No! I mean, I noticed you because I noticed Billie in her hat and…"

CRINKLES

I stopped when I saw he was grinning and quirked one eyebrow at him.

"Don't let it go to your head."

The plane jolted and dropped and then dropped some more. I grabbed at the armrest and realised I was clutching his hand instead. Which would have been embarrassing except I was too scared to care, the fear pulsing in me like a monster, making my stomach twist itself in knots.

"Oh, crap. Crap, crap, crap."

He squeezed my hand and the pressure was good, helping me focus.

"Just listen to my voice, okay? Tell me about your sister. What's her name?"

I tried to make my brain work but it was paralysed. It wasn't a hard question though. Surely I knew the answer.

"Sam. It's Sam."

"Great. And did you have a nickname for her growing up?"

I tried to smile. It came out as more of a grimace. "Sister Sam when we were little. And then probably bitch when we were teenagers."

He laughed and I felt the panic trickle away slightly.

"And was that her at the airport?"

I nodded. "It was the first anniversary of her divorce so I

wanted to be there for her."

"What was her ex like?"

I frowned. "Okay. I mean, nice enough. They just weren't really suited."

"And what about you? Boyfriend or husband waiting for you in Sydney?"

I shook my head, clutching his hand again as more turbulence hit.

"Imogen?"

"No. No partner. Not for over a year."

He smiled and my heart did the quick step again. My brain was a confused mess, caught somewhere between fear and attraction. It was... distracting. Maybe this is what I needed every time I flew. A cute guy to distract me.

"Well, that's good to know." He squeezed my hand slightly, his thumb rubbing across the top of my fingers, and the lower half of my body turned to molten lava. I licked my lips, trying to get some moisture in my suddenly dry mouth.

"Are you flirting with me to distract me?"

᎒᎒᎒

My grin got bigger. "No, I'm flirting with you because you're beautiful. And the hand holding's a bonus. But is it working anyway?"

I couldn't believe I'd actually said that. She was just looking at me though, like her brain was still too panicked to think.

"Is what working?"

"Am I distracting you?" My voice was rough – like my desire was on display. Christ! Her breath caught but I didn't know what that meant.

"Yes."

It was amazing that one word could almost undo me. And then the attendant asked if we wanted food, breaking the moment, and Imogen took her hand from mine. For a second, I wondered if it was wrong to grab it back. Yep, definitely wrong.

I massaged my fingers instead, trying to get rid of the feeling of loss. I'd never felt like this before. Especially after only – I checked my watch – half an hour. Half an hour! Scary. Scary and exciting and fantastic and confusing. I didn't understand what the hell was going on here.

❧

He moved his hand back to his lap and I watched him rub his fingers. Crap, he'd think I was looking at his crotch.

And now I actually was!

God, look away, Imogen! I turned to the window, trying to distract myself.

"So, what do you do for work?" His voice was casual, like he had it all together, unlike me. But when I looked back, he was still massaging his fingers.

Work. Good. Safe topic.

"I'm a graphic artist. How about you?"

"Psychologist."

"Oh no. And you get stuck next to the only lunatic on the plane!"

He laughed. "Fear of flying doesn't make you a lunatic. That's my professional diagnosis." He took a deep breath. "But you could pay me back for the consultation by having a drink with me while we're waiting for the next flight."

Yes. The word was desperately trying to push its way out. But I had to think. Think about... I didn't know what I was supposed to think about.

"Okay. That would be nice."

And he let out his breath. Interesting.

For the rest of the flight, we talked. Talked about everything and nothing. Laughing. Teasing. And it was easy. Easier than it'd ever been before, even with my anxiety keeping me company. I hoped he was feeling the same.

"Cabin crew, prepare for landing."

Shit. Shit, shit, shit. Landing was the worst part. And I had another flight after this. Why didn't I drive?

Chris touched my wrist, moving the bracelet slightly. My skin tingled, the nerve endings feeling like they had a direct line to my stomach.

"Tell me what the bracelet's for again?"

"Safe travel."

"Right. And good luck?"

I nodded, eyes closed, trying not to listen to the whine of the engines as we started our descent. Trying not to listen to the wheels lock into place. Trying to ignore all of it.

I felt him take my hand again and gratitude washed over me. It helped. God knows why, but his touch helped.

"And do you think it's brought you good luck so far?"

I opened my eyes. He was watching me, eyes serious, and the feeling in my stomach travelled lower.

◌⃝⃝

"Yes."

Damn, just looking at her now, lips slightly parted, I wanted to kiss her. And not a nice, polite kiss. A hot one, pulling her hard against me. Everything in me clenched tight and I wondered who I was for a moment. Where was the calm, controlled, rational Chris my sister was always accusing me of being?

The wheels touched down. A perfect landing. I hadn't even

noticed. She let out a shaky laugh and I rubbed my thumb over the inside of her wrist, watching as she nervously licked her lips. Christ!

The plane stopped and I stood, keeping the space in front of me for her to get out. All I could think about was her, almost touching me, the heat of her, the feeling of protection that loomed up in me. Even though she didn't need it. Even though I'd never felt like this before. Except now. With her.

She smiled at me as we walked through the airport and I felt like I was floating. And then we paid for drinks and settled into a booth, the lighting dim. My heart was beating against my ribs like it was trying to send her a Morse code message.

I played with the condensation on my glass, trying to sort out what was going on in my head and how I could say the words without coming across like a total weirdo. I could feel her watching me. And I could feel her own nervousness.

"You know, if you want to have a drink and then go, that's okay."

She looked worried I might say yes, but maybe that was wishful thinking. I took a deep breath, hoping I wasn't making an idiot of myself.

"The crazy thing is, I don't want this to finish. I like you. And I've never felt like this before. Does that make you want to run?"

Her beautiful brown eyes were calm as she looked at me. "No, actually. It doesn't."

"Really?"

"Really."

೦੩୫౭

He smiled and brought my hand up to kiss my fingers. It was the sexiest thing that had happened to me in a long time and every organ in my body seemed to react. Then he leant closer, hesitating, a breath away from me. I reached up, lacing my hand through the hair at the nape of his neck like I'd imagined doing for the whole flight, and pulled him to me. His lips were gentle and his tongue flicked my lip, tasting me, until I felt like I was going to explode. I pulled him closer still, wanting more, and he moaned. Holy crap. I needed to stop. We were in public. I sat back and he looked at me, eyes wide.

"Wow." He reached out to touch my lip with his thumb and I gently bit it. Bit it! I'd never done that on a first date. If that's what this even was.

"You know, I think I might need some professional support on the next flight." My voice was embarrassingly husky.

He smiled, a lazy one that spoke of wanting and lust.

"I'm happy to help."

And all I could think was that tiger's eyes were definitely bringers of good luck.

5

SUNSET ON STONE

SUZIE JAY

Kit Welsh rushed through the door of Freddy's Jewellery Store in time to see her boss digging at the edge of a gemstone, before the stone flipped into the air and came down with a clang. The stone spun across the floor and came to a stop against Kit's shoe. It looked as if it was going to be another interesting day at work.

Kit bent to retrieve the gem and held it up to the light. It wasn't the nicest she'd ever seen. Streaks of yellow and auburn all the way through to tan and mustard gleamed across the stone. Shrugging, she held it out to her boss.

"Here you go, Freddy."

Freddy glanced at the gemstone through his oversized glasses. He looked like an owl who'd just pecked on a lemon. "Throw it in the bin. It's a tiger's eye. They're practically worthless. The diamonds surrounding it, however, are extremely valuable." He dropped his head once again to work on the brooch, popping out one precious diamond after another.

"Would it be alright if I keep it?" There was something about the chunky stone that resonated with her. Maybe it was because she knew how it felt to be passed over in favour of a greater beauty.

"Keep it, bury it, use it to pitch at the heads of your enemies, I don't care. Just get it away from me and my diamonds."

Kit smiled and stuffed it into her purse, then prepared herself for the workday ahead. "What's on the agenda today?" she asked, as she secured an apron around her waist.

"I'll need a new setting for these diamonds. Something sleek and modern. I'm thinking along the lines of a drop pendant for five of them and this bigger one might make a nice solitaire ring." Freddy held it in the air to examine it closer. "Yes. Definitely a star on its own."

Kit scraped her auburn hair up into a ponytail and picked up her loupe. Staring at the largest diamond, she wondered who on earth would cluster a diamond of such quality with a tiger's eye. Freddy was right to suggest a solitaire. She placed it on the scale. Just over one and a half carats. Two of the others were a perfect one carat and would make great earrings, leaving the three smaller ones for the drop pendant.

Kit ran the idea past Freddy, who pushed his glasses to the top of his head causing his curly grey hair to stick out in all directions. "Great idea. That is why I pay you the big bucks."

"Just a smidgen more than minimum wage actually."

"Pfft." The elderly man dismissed her comment with a wave of his hand and Kit sniggered.

Her wage wasn't too bad, but they both knew she could

make almost double that in the city. She told people she stayed because Freddy needed her but, if she were honest with herself, it might have more to do with someone else.

Besides, her job was satisfactory.

In fact, every aspect of her life was satisfactory. Except one.

‍‍‍
CR80

"Hey Joe. Been busy?"

Joe glanced up from pouring beer and smiled at the sight of Kit. Her shock of bright red hair fizzed out around her face, framing her piercing blue eyes. His heart beat faster and he gulped back the dryness taking over his throat.

"You're here early. I thought you'd still be at w—woah." He'd forgotten to stop pouring. Now the beer and drip tray in front of him were overflowing onto the counter.

"Here." Kit stretched across the bar. Her breasts squashed against the counter as she grabbed for a dishcloth and threw it over the expanding puddle. He reluctantly drew his eyes from her.

Joe pulled his apron over his head before beer soaked through to his shirt. Why did he always feel like a gangly teen when she was around? Although, he was usually better at hiding it.

"Hang on." With an apologetic shrug he wiped the dripping beer and delivered it to his customer before he rushed back to Kit. Her visits were weekly at best, and he never had her company for long.

"Now, what can I get you?" he asked, his suaveness back.

"A bottle of champagne and two glasses. Thanks." As she smiled up at him a cute little dimple formed in her left cheek. He had to look away. She was too endearing. If he stared for too long, he'd be rendered useless. "I'm meeting Bridget."

"Celebrating?"

"Not really." She shrugged and he stared at her, waiting. "Just my twenty-ninth birthday." Her skin tinted a flattering shade of pink.

"That's not nothing! That's indeed something." He pushed a bottle towards her. "On the house. Consider it a birthday gift."

Her hand stopped short of grabbing the bottle. "Joe, you don't have to do that."

"Come on now. It's a bottle of alcohol and I own a bar. It's hardly a grand gesture." He spun to grab the glasses. When he turned back, she had the champagne tucked under her arm. "Get settled and I'll bring out an ice-bucket."

"Thank you. You've always been a wonderful friend to me." His heart sunk to the deepest, darkest pit of his stomach. He'd been friend-zoned. Any man on earth could tell you the friend zone was locked down tighter than Alcatraz. Once you were in, it was practically impossible to escape.

CRBO

Kit began to twist the cork but stopped as a wave of bravery swept through her. Birthdays were meant to be exciting after all. She spun back on her heel and leaned over the counter, dropping a kiss on Joe's cheek. "Thanks again. If you get a chance later, come and have a drink with us, won't you?"

Joe smiled, revealing a row of perfectly straight teeth. "I'll try." He threw her a wink and her feet practically melted into the floor. He dashed off to serve a customer at the other end of the bar. Customers moved all around him, but she only saw Joe.

After three years of friendship she had no misconceptions that they'd ever be more than that. She should try to get over her crush. Besides, she was certain her friend Bridget had a thing for Joe as well.

As if her thoughts had summoned her, Bridget threw open the doors and sashayed into the bar. Her gaze darted about the room before it finally settled on Kit. Flicking of strands her waist length blonde hair over her shoulder, she waved. Bridget had won the genetic lottery with her model looks, naturally sleek hair and gorgeous caramel skin. Kit glanced down at her own pale skin, her arms covered in a smattering of freckles.

She suppressed the tiny insecure voice inside her. Today was her birthday, and the man she liked had just given her a bottle of champagne. She would focus on that.

The sight of each man's jaw dropping as Bridget made her way across the floor was like watching the Mexican wave at a football match. But Bridget didn't pay attention, instead going straight to Kit and embracing her in a warm hug. "Happy birthday, gorgeous. You look amazing in that dress. Doesn't she look great Joe?"

From the other end of the bar Joe ran an assessing eye over Kit and gave a thumbs up.

"Now, let's get drunk and forget our problems."

"What problems could you possibly have?" Kit teased her.

Bridget sighed dramatically. "I lost my job."

"Again?" Kit clamped a hand across her mouth, hoping it hadn't sounded too harsh. She lowered her tone. "That's the fourth in as many months."

Bridget shrugged off her coat and flopped down onto a stool. "I know. I guess I'm just no good with authority."

Joe leaned over the bar. "That's code for being a brat," he teased.

Bridget narrowed her eyes in mock offence. "I'm not *that* bad. I just like to get my own way."

"Bridget you're perfect just as you are. You shouldn't change for anyone." Kit laughed.

"I really am, aren't I?"

It was a statement, not a question and, although Kit knew Bridget was joking, she was well aware her friend meant every word.

"Joe, you got any jobs going?" Bridget asked in her sweetest, honey-dripping voice.

Kit giggled at the look of horror on Joe's face.

"Yes, we have jobs. But not for you." He hurried away to serve a customer.

"Why do you hurt me like this, Joe? You know I only have love for you," Bridget yelled after him and gripped her heart dramatically. She held her pose for a few seconds before turning back to Kit. "He's so sexy and he doesn't even know it."

Kit watched Joe at the opposite end of the bar. He *was* sexy.

So sexy. But he was also incredibly sweet and funny. "I don't really see the appeal," she lied.

Bridget grabbed Kit's shoulder, spinning Kit's stool to face her. "You lying little wench. *Everyone* can see his appeal."

"Maybe, if you like your men tall, toned and tattooed." She stifled a fake yawn for good measure.

Bridget rolled her eyes. "As I said, *everyone*! I don't know why you two don't just get together already."

"Because we're friends. Besides, if you like him so much, why don't you date him?" Her mouth dried as she struggled to get the words out. She always did this. Sabotaged herself by stepping away from what she really wanted.

"Oh, I've tried." Bridget sighed and dragged her gaze away from Joe's tight backside.

The blood drained from Kit's face and the pulse in her neck thundered. "You have?" she squeaked, her words barely audible.

"God, yes. Every time I see him."

Kit froze while her brain whirled, attempting to find an acceptable response. But it was all she could manage not to be sick. She'd been right. Bridget *did* have a thing for Joe.

Somewhere on the path between despair and darkness she became aware of Bridget watching her. Assessing her. She plastered a smile on her face. "You'd make a great couple." She was talking too fast and, with each additional word that tumbled from her lips, her friend's eyes narrowed further.

"Pity he has no interest in me."

Kit let out a sigh and the coil in her stomach released a little.

"His heart lies elsewhere. In fact, I'm trying to set him up with a wonderful friend of mine," Bridget added with a glint in her eye.

Kit realised immediately that Bridget was referring to her and the coil sprang back, tighter than ever. But this time it was because her friend was relentless and if she'd decided that Kit and Joe should be together, she wouldn't give up until complete embarrassment had been endured.

∞

"Cute guy at ten o'clock." Bridget pulled a compact from her purse and flipped it open. She batted her lips together and smiled. Snapping the mirror closed, she placed it on the bar next to her. "He looks rich too. That suit's been fitted."

The man in question adjusted his tie. As he did, the sleeves of his jacket inched up, revealing a gold watch.

"That watch looks like a real Rolex," Kit added.

The man in the suit strolled over and leaned between Kit and Bridget. He had his back to Kit, which was something she'd become accustomed to, over the years. The fact that Bridget hadn't already been whisked away tonight by some prince charming was surprising. Although, according to Bridget, they all ended up frogs in the end.

Kit stared at the pleat in the back of the man's pinstripe suit while he worked his magic, charming Bridget right off her bar stool. Bridget stood and poked her head around the man's torso.

"Look, I know it's your birthday Kitty Kat, but it is getting late. You wouldn't mind if I popped out for a quick drink with..." She glanced up at the man.

"Peter," he said, his voice deep and smooth.

Kit leaned in and spoke softly, "Be good."

"Stop trying to ruin all my fun." Bridget quirked her eyebrow. "And Kitty, don't walk home alone."

"I'm fine. Really. I'll leave soon."

"Joe," Bridget called out, her eyes sparkling. "Walk Kitty home, will you? I'm trusting you with her welfare."

Joe glanced up from the glass he was drying and nodded to Bridget. His gaze crept over, locked with Kit's and he smiled.

"Maybe give her a kiss at the door. It is her birthday after all." Bridget slipped into her jacket and curled her arm through Peter's. "Ta, ta sweetie. Happy birthday."

Kit's skin burned as she stared after Bridget's retreating back and swaying hips until the doors closed behind her. She couldn't bear to look at Joe.

"Definitely a star on her own," Kit whispered, shaking her head.

"You say star, I say pain in the arse. Tomato, tomato."

She spun at the sound of Joe's voice and found he was now perched on the bar stool next to hers.

"It's just something Freddy said earlier." Relieved to change the focus from what Bridget had just said, she continued. "Some gems are destined to be stars on their own. Bridget definitely falls under that category."

His chestnut eyes softened. "She has to be a star on her own, no other self-respecting star would put up with her."

Despite her embarrassment at Bridget's shameless attempt to push her and Joe together, she laughed. The snippy banter between her two friends always kept her entertained, if not insanely jealous.

"It'd be nice to be noticed sometimes." She sighed and then gasped when she realised that she'd said it out loud and in front of Joe, of all people.

"Seems like you might be the lone star." He squeezed her shoulder and indicated the empty seat where Bridget had been sitting. "Here, pour me a drink."

She did as he asked and they clinked their glasses together, like two fizzy little heads bowing to each other.

"Happy birthday to me." She smiled, trying to make an effort to be cheery.

"Happy birthday to you, gorgeous." His voice was low and husky. Like a late-night radio host, designed to lull you into slumber. Although his had the opposite effect and a thrill ran down her spine.

"Joe, you don't have to walk me home. Once I've finished this champagne, I can walk by myself."

Joe leaned in close, his face just inches from hers. Her skin tingled as if a thousand butterflies were dancing over her bare arms. "I *want* to walk you home."

She knew she was blushing, but there was nothing she could do about it. She was staring at a spot on the bar, trying to slow her racing heart when she spotted Bridget's compact. She picked it up and cursed her hands for shaking under his gaze.

She popped the clip on her clutch and it fell open. The tiger's eye Freddy had discarded slid onto the bar with a clang.

Joe retrieved it, examining the stone in his hand. He turned it this way and that, allowing the light to caress it. "Pretty stone."

"Not really. It's fairly plain."

"So why are you carrying it around in your purse?"

There was no way to explain herself without sounding pathetically ridiculous. "It was the ugly duckling cast aside by Freddy, made me feel kind of bad for it. I know it's an inanimate object, but there was a sort of kinship."

He stared at the stone closer. "I can see the resemblance." She smiled, expecting him to make some joke about having rocks in her head or some such thing. "You both have the same auburn colouring and are both stunningly beautiful."

She looked up from the stone and found his warm eyes waiting. There was no hint of teasing or mocking. Her heart hammered, determined to be noticed, against her chest.

She drew her gaze from his and rushed to change the subject. "It's just an old stone. I should've let Freddy throw it out. I don't know why I collect all this rubbish."

He placed his hand on hers and, as she registered the contact, she stopped talking.

"If you look closely, it almost looks like a sunset. Don't you think?"

She stared at it. The stone instantly transformed in her perception. How had she not noticed that before? "How do you do that? You look at something as plain as this stone and see something exquisite? Or you look at me and call me gorgeous." She hadn't wanted to let her insecurities slip out, but curiosity got the better of her.

"Fiery red hair, like a campfire in the night, set off by eyes of the palest blue. You're practically a human unicorn." The line would have sounded corny coming from any other lips, but when Joe spoke them, her heart jumped to life.

She struggled to speak, every cell in her body seemed to vibrate in anticipation. "A unicorn? Really, Joe? More like a plain old horse." Her words came out thick, as though her throat was coated in syrup.

"Red hair and blue eyes are the rarest of all combinations. Sometimes, it takes every bit of will power I have to not stare at you. You're like the tiger's eye. The longer I look, the more beauty presents itself."

He removed his hand from hers and the absence of his touch left her feeling incomplete. But he reached out and ran his finger down the side of her cheek, tracing along her jaw. A shiver ripped through Kit and it seemed completely natural to tilt her chin up and press her lips against Joe's.

When he took her face in his hands and returned her kiss, it was the best birthday present she could imagine.

6

BOUNCING THE BUSTLE

MARYANNE ROSS

L ilwen felt like a fool. It wasn't as though she had shillings to spare. She felt on the verge of something: finally able to leap into a new life that was hers alone... if only she had the courage. She wanted some kind of affirmation. Someone telling her what she wanted to hear.

The fortune teller's tent was striped red and dusty black, small and lushly decorated. Warm and intimate inside, with plump, richly embroidered cushions strewn throughout. Lilwen sat at a low table, watching the hawk-nosed woman bent over the gorgeously painted cards, faded and creased in the places where her fingers touched.

"You wish for adventure. You must find your courage."

Well, she knew that! She didn't need to waste a shilling to discover that!

"Let the eye of the tiger guide you," the fortune teller had said in her creaking voice, her dark eyes sly and amused.

≪≫

Lilwen had forgotten about it until now. She was trying to ignore the itchy heat of her mourning costume in the strong January sun, while she stared in fascination at the tiger at the Melbourne Zoo.

The beast strolled through its cage, an image of grace and lethal beauty, its flicking and twitching tail a sign of its restlessness. She sighed. She knew that restlessness. She had foolishly thought that with her twenties would come resignation and acceptance of dull routine.

The beast met her gaze. His clear amber eyes glowed bright with intelligence and suffering. The animal's gaze was so intense, Lilwen stepped back: straight into a hard body behind her!

Two strong hands encircled her small but uncorseted waist – she could feel their warmth through her bodice, her petticoat, her slip... on her skin. She gasped.

She was immediately conscious of her dress: her hair, sweaty in the heat of the day under her desperately modish new hat; her high buttoned bodice, dark for mourning and for practicality both, with its rows of pearl buttons and a frivolous suggestion of a frill. Her long skirt, swishing unhampered around her hips and legs.

She swivelled and looked up, embarrassed, and the apology died on her lips. It was as though she looked into the tiger's eye once more: dark honey, fiercely intelligent; dangerous, predatory, self-contained. Dark brown curling hair, streaked gold by the sun. Strong nose, firm mouth.

His clothes exaggerated his feral, feline quality. A disreputable hat, its brim creased over the right eye. His fawn coloured overcoat was long and worn open, hanging from broad shoulders and a robust torso. His dark brown leather boots were soft with wear, but well-cared for. His general appearance presented a kind of dishevelled grace. His expression was sardonic, amused. He smelled of leather and clean sweat.

"Tyger, tyger, burning bright." His voice was contained strength, rumbling deep and low in his chest. Lilwen almost imagined his tail swishing behind him.

She wriggled a little to evade his grasp, but those long-fingered hands tightened on her waist. Not so tight that she couldn't break free, more of an invitation, a firm caress. For one long moment, Lilwen remained within the tiger's grasp, transfixed by the tiger's eye.

"I thought all the beasts were safely in their cages," she said, looking directly into that amber gaze.

The surprised laugh burst out of him, crinkling his eyes and stretching his wide mouth. He grinned down at her. "I never did enjoy cages, my lady. Or tolerate any form of restriction."

Lilwen gave a small, involuntary moan of desire. "Oh how I agree with you!" Then, feeling she had sounded a little mad, she continued, "That is, women have so many cages, layers and layers of them. You burst out of one, only to find there is a bigger one around that, and a yet bigger one around that one too."

The tiger took her arm, placed it in his, and began to stroll with her around the shady landscaped gardens.

"So you have been bursting your stays?" he asked conversationally. Lilwen blushed, stopped. She took a breath. She knew he had felt the soft pliancy of skin and muscle rather than a corset.

She felt reckless. This half-savage stranger seemed so far beyond the pale that honesty, for once, seemed not only possible, but exciting, daring, real.

"As you no doubt felt as you laid hands on me just now. While my father lay ill, I bounced my mini-bustle down the cellar stairs. When he died, I crushed my corsets."

The tiger's deep laugh rumbled through him again. "And may one enquire, has there been a corresponding release of social behaviours?" Lilwen shot him a look. The corners of his wide mouth were pressed in. Those dark honey eyes had mischief lurking in their depths.

She said, serious now, "Changing my dress seemed right: the first step to adventure, to finally being my own woman, as the new century throws off the shadow of the old. Australia has become a Federation and the old queen has given way to a new monarch. There will be universal suffrage, perhaps." She paused, wriggling as a trickle of sweat crept inside her bodice. "I fear that long habits of obedience are not easily broken. Sadly, I am entirely respectable."

"Then the respectable thing for me to do, having so mishandled you, would be to procure you refreshment. No doubt you enjoy those foolish ices?"

"No doubt! But what luxury, Sir."

Sitting at a tiny iron-work table, trying to eat their ices with a modicum of manners, the tiger told her his name: Sawyer Thane. "Lilwen Jones," he repeated hers, drawing out the syllables, his lips pouting on the 'w'.

This man was not tame, Lilwen thought. Not this vital man, with his air of danger, of fast reflexes and instant activity. He wore his freedom as carelessly as his hat. She couldn't stop looking at him.

Normally, she would have lowered her eyes; kept an outward semblance of virtue and modesty. She had long ago learnt to hide her blaze of intelligence, and her impatience with the littleness of women's days.

"Perhaps you are an explorer?" she asked. Her heart quickened within her. "I can hardly think of a life more exciting. To see all those far-flung countries. To brave the forests of the Americas, to visit the beautiful gardens and forests of the Far East, to see first-hand the strange animals of Indo-China."

"You are interested in explorers' tales?"

"No!" Lilwen, laughed, blushed. "That is, yes." She fiddled with the tiny spoon. "I wish to be an explorer myself – of a kind." He was silent. She risked a glance up: his face bore no judgement, no conventional shock. His deep amber eyes were fixed on hers. A strange expression was enlivening his countenance. Wonder? Hope? She felt something thaw deep inside.

"A plant collector," she whispered, breathlessly. There. It was spoken. It was real. She gazed at him, almost desperately wanting affirmation. "To travel to distant lands, collecting plants I have never before seen, in places one must have desperate courage to venture. I wish... I wish I was that person. Could be that person."

"How very unusual you are, Miss Lilwen Jones. May I ask what is stopping you? Apart from society's certain disapproval?"

"So like a man!" Lilwen laughed, and his fierce grin warmed her through. "I have worked for years in my father's plant nursery, since he lost nearly everything in the crashes of '93. I adore plants, but as I tend them, they…"

"Yes?" He was leaning forward, one long brown curl covering his left cheek, causing him to tilt his head as he regarded her. A long finger hooked the errant curl back behind his ear. His hands, his fingers, Lilwen thought. So different from other men's manicured, cultivated hands.

"My plants speak to me," she confessed. She took a breath. "Oh not literally, of course, but as I stroke their shining leaves, and touch their velvety petals, nurture their soft new furry shoots, they whisper to me of exotic locales, climes far away, of adventure and strange peoples."

"Travelling can be very rugged."

"Do you think I don't know?" she retorted. "Mr Partridge has sat at our table many times, recounting exciting tales of his youth. He was a famous botanist and explorer, you know. But what is your work?"

"I fear you would not approve, should I tell you what it is."

"And why should you care about my approval, Sir?"

"Perhaps your fascination with my tiger has given me pause."

He stared at her steadily, narrowing his eyes as though making a decision. "My work is not respectable. I catch wildlife for zoological gardens, here and around the world."

There was a long pause. Lilwen slammed down the remains of her ice. Stared at him. Felt something rising from her gullet and choking her throat. Horror. Disappointment. Disgust.

"You are a *poacher*? You catch these magnificent animals,

and then... and then... *imprison* them? And you were laughing at my talk of women's cages and prisons?"

Sawyer stood up. "Lilwen, no! Not at..."

Lilwen stood too. She smacked a coin onto the table. It bounced and fell off. She noted with a pang that it was a whole shilling, too much for a small refreshment, but she was so enraged and disappointed, she simply could not bend and retrieve it.

"A hunter!" she hissed. "Debasing those proud, wild, free animals."

She spat on the ground, in probably the most unfeminine exhibition of behaviour she had indulged in since she was two years old. "That's what I think of your ice! That's what I think of your work. It's cruel, and wrong."

Sawyer stretched out a long, tanned arm.

Lilwen felt unaccountable tears rising in her throat, burning the backs of her eyes. She turned and strode off, dodging in and out of the shrubberies, like a demented child; she was so anguished. She heard him coming after her, calling her. He could track wild animals, of course he would find her.

She went where even no half-civilised man would go, and retired to the ladies' ablutions.

CRBD

Much later, Lilwen sat in her tiny kitchen, toying with her small plain meal. For just a few minutes life had ripped into vivid colour: full of possibility and adventure. Meeting the man-tiger had made her crazy dreams seem not impossible. An explorer, she had thought. A plant collector.

But what was she really? A child of 1880s Marvellous Melbourne, that decade of gold, glitz, and glamour. Then, when the great bust came in the 90s, the banks shut their doors on their screaming investors, everything turning to dust.

She had to forgo her governess and work instead at the nursery that kept her and her father alive. Her father, twisted and bitter with his loss of fortune, bullied his wife into an early grave and terrorised Lilwen, his only child, into a dull submission to labour.

She had been saved by the plants. Rich red petals and dark bamboo stems telling tales of tropical climates; glossy leaves and intricate flowers singing of their rainforest home; heavy perfumes and golden stamens swollen with pollen and pulsing with yearning.

Her father would not listen when she urged him, again and again, to consider collecting new plants, for it could turn their fortunes around once again.

Finally, that sour carping man died. She found his stash of sovereigns under the bed.

She was free. She had stood there, allowing the golden cascade to run streaming through her hands onto the floor, laughing out loud, quite madly, letting the fancies long since repressed come flying back into her fevered mind.

Quite soon, she discovered acid truths. One, money disappeared fast. Two, ignorance: how did one become an explorer?

Three, she lacked the courage. Her commonsense, which

had kept them alive, kept them going, was a snare for her dreams now. She could only fear; could only think of all the problems: what if she spent all her money without collecting new plants, what would happen to her? What terrible things could happen to a young woman alone? She knew, of course. All women did.

She had better think instead about getting a husband. Lilwen sighed. A merchant had long been expressing clumsy interest. He was two decades older than she, fat and jowly, with a wet mouth.

Mr Partridge, the aging botanist, was also showing interest. He had invited her to a society ball. Such pleasures had often been denied her: her father, she realised now, had not wanted to lose his workhorse.

✀

At the ball, Lilwen danced twice with Mr Partridge who then popped a cool beaded glass of sparkling wine into her hand. He had hold of her arm and was steering her towards a convenient alcove. She glanced at his smug expression. A pair of honey tiger-eyes flashed in her mind. She repressed the vision, and realised Mr Partridge had been speaking. "So naturally, as my wife, you will continue to oversee the plant nursery, without sullying those lovely hands any further..."

"Mr Partridge!" Lilwen realised with horror that it would be the height of impoliteness to reveal she hadn't even been listening to his proposal of marriage! She couldn't very well ask him to repeat it.

"Mr Partridge... the greatest desire of my heart is to travel, as you did in your youth..." Oh dear, she thought. That wasn't very well said, reminding him of his years. "Travel. Collecting plants..."

"Nonsense!" he cut her off. "You will be more comfortable in my manor. With plenty of *other* nursery work in the future, I pray!" He positively leered.

Lilwen felt her fabulous new life fading to beige. A bright coal of survival stirred to flame within her.

"Sir. I am honoured by your proposal, but it appears you expect me to go on as I have before! What then, is the advantage of the married state to me? Currently, I have a little money, I have autonomy and can order my days as I wish."

Mr Partridge's face purpled. "I had not thought you so! To go on in this unwomanly way – it must be grief!"

"Oh aye," Lilwen said, "Tis certainly grief – sorrow that I had not fought for my true wishes long before this!" She shook him off, ran across the ballroom and into the garden, lit for the evening with hanging lamps and candles, creating a magical, golden paradise.

As she stood there, her chest heaving with emotion and a kind of unfurling elation, Lilwen saw a figure striped in golden light and deep shadow, stalking through the bushes. She knew that loping pace, that easy manner. Sawyer, here?

Lilwen's heartbeat accelerated. She was outwardly respectable. No wonder poor Mr Partridge laboured under a misapprehension – but inside! Oh inside! How her traitorous heart leapt at the sight of Sawyer striding towards her.

"Do not importune me, Sir! I am labouring under strong emotion – anger – forbidden to the female sex! You must leave me to eat my chagrin and swallow it down in pieces, like a good woman."

"Again? But indeed, there is nothing better than indulging in a lovely fit of choler once in a while!"

Lilwen laughed.

He stepped close. He was a creature made of the lantern's glow and shifting shadows. He placed his hands around her waist. Lilwen's skin remembered his touch: the heat and strength in his hands. The delicate, questioning touch of his fingers. Her body shifted closer. She must be holding her breath; it was difficult to get sufficient air. Their eyes locked. Her emotions were in tumult. She felt anxious, disturbed, fascinated, yet somehow... *safe*.

"Lilwen," he said. She opened her mouth. He stared at her lips. In the darkness, his head came closer. His lips grazed hers. "I have been waiting for you."

She thought of a tiger hunting its prey: concentrated grace and total focus on the object of its desire, and shivered. Deliciously.

"Stalking me, Sir? I am not one of your unfortunate beasts, to be hunted and trapped in a cage for your amusement!" Her voice was a squeak.

"Lilwen, please listen." He put gentle hands on either side of her face. "I save animals that are injured or sick. They would die if left in the wild. The zoos care for them and keep them safe."

Lilwen's mind reeled. Her mental image of him shifted.

Sawyer said, "My work is perilous. Wildlife poaching is worth much money. It involves desperate, dangerous men."

"So you, too, say my work is no activity for a woman." Lilwen was surprised by the surge of bitter feeling this gave her, as though Sawyer had betrayed her.

"It depends on the woman." Sawyer's smile glowed in the golden lamplight. "Lilwen Jones, I DARE you to explore with me, if that is the desire of your heart. I have no wish to see a brave female pacing and chewing at her cages."

She stared at him, her world spinning with pieces of coloured glass, coming together in a fabulous design.

Sawyer searched in his pocket. Held out a ring. The stone flickered brown and amber in the lamplight.

"How lovely," Lilwen breathed.

Sawyer took her hand. "The gem is called tiger's eye. It gives Emotional Healing, Career Success, Courage, and... Passion in the Loins!"

His eyes burned as he slid the ring onto her finger. "I chose it because you loved my tiger. And because... you would give me all this. I never dreamed..." He swallowed hard. He growled, "I find I love you. Could you, perhaps...?"

"I do already," Lilwen replied, laughing as Sawyer grabbed her, swinging her in the air, and kissing her lips with savage abandon.

⚬⚭⚬

Before they set sail, Sawyer and Lilwen were married. Lilwen's heart leapt within her as she heard the words marking the start of her greatest adventure: her very own tiger's 'aye'.

7

THE TIGER'S EYES

CAROLINE DENESS

Bath   1818

"**L**ord Marston." Lucilla curtsied as the tall, contained gentleman turned and bowed. He seemed to dwarf the parlour in Miss Brodie's School for Young Ladies where Lucilla taught.

"Forgive the intrusion, Miss Creed, but I am afraid I am the bearer of sad news. Your grandmother passed away overnight." His serious dark eyes searched her face.

"Oh no, I've been so worried. Grandmama looked incredibly sad as she said goodbye to me last Sunday." Lucilla's big grey eyes shimmered, and Lord Marston prayed she wouldn't cry.

"My mother hopes I can persuade you to come back with me to discuss the funeral. This is for you as well. It was on her desk."

Marston handed her a note with Lucilla's name written in a

spidery hand. He was relieved to see Miss Creed holding her emotions in check; brave as well as blessed with the serene face he had admired when visiting his mother.

Lucilla, pocketing the note, was reassured by the strength in Lord Marston's arm and by the sympathy in his caramel gaze as he escorted her to his curricle. He had always seemed like a distant god when she had seen him as she visited her grandmother: his face like a classical statue, framed by dark waving hair.

Grandmama, a distant cousin of Lady Marston, had been living with her as a sort of companion since Lucilla's parents had moved to India while Lucilla was a pupil at the school. Lucilla had continued on as a teacher at the school after her parents and her young brother had succumbed, tragically, to a virulent fever sweeping Bengal.

CRO

It wasn't until a weary Lucilla reached her bedchamber that evening and opened her grandmother's last note, that she was overcome by loneliness. The last person she loved, gone. Would she ever get away from the school now?

Trying to decipher the scratchy writing through her tears, Lucilla found the words 'tiger's eye' and a vision of her Gran's brooch intruded. The rippled bands of yellow shining from the otherwise mud brown stone had intrigued rather than attracted Lucilla.

'You'll find your fortune in the tiger's eyes. It was due to come to you when you turned twenty-one but it seems I won't live to see that special day. I'm so sorry.'

Fighting more tears, Lucilla considered the note. It didn't make sense: for a start there was only one brooch, and the stone was only semi-precious, as far as Lucilla knew. She would discuss it with Lady Marston when they sorted through Gran's room after the funeral.

CR80

Lucilla managed to contain her tears during the moving service at the Abbey, and as she received condolences at the small gathering in Lady Marston's drawing room. But, when she surveyed her grandmother's sitting room and bedroom, the tears quietly fell.

Tactfully, Lady Marston placed a handkerchief in Lucilla's hand and excused herself to speak with the housekeeper.

"Just look through her things and think about what you would like to keep."

Nodding, Lucilla moved blindly to sit at the dressing table and opened an ornate box to search for the brooch.

CR80

Hugh, Lord Marston, found her thus sometime later: sitting staring at a piece of jewellery. His heart faltered to see the lost expression on the normally calm or even amused face. He felt himself falling into the grey pools of her eyes. *Good God*.

"Miss Creed, my mother sent me to ask if you'd like to join us for tea?"

Lucilla sat, staring at his concerned face, gradually noting his rather endearing frown.

"Why would she say 'my fortune's in the tiger's eyes'? I'm sure this brooch is not seriously precious?" Lucilla's parents had gone to India for her father to make his fortune with The East India Company, but there had been little to salvage after their deaths.

Hugh stirred from his trance to take the brooch Lucilla held towards him. The touch of her fingers sent heat up his arm and he raised surprised eyes to her enquiring gaze, noting her slightly parted pink lips on the way.

Getting a grip on himself, Hugh stepped back and cast a practised eye over the semi-precious stone.

"I have to agree with your assessment, Miss Creed. Was there something with this?"

"No, and I've looked through all her drawers in here." Lucilla stood and walked through to the other room. "I can't think of anything else Grandmama ever mentioned being valuable."

As they stood and surveyed the other room, Hugh noted a tiger skin over the back of a day bed.

"Are tiger skins valuable? I've seen the odd one in mansions." Hugh crossed to the skin and lifted it to check its condition. As he did so, the sunlight from the window reflected through the tiger's yellow eyes.

"Oh," Lucilla gasped. "It almost looks alive in the sunshine."

Instead of shock, Hugh felt a shiver of suspicion as he brought the tiger's head closer to inspect the eyes.

"Humph."

"What does that mean Lord Marston?" Lucilla looked hopefully at this reassuringly strong man.

"It means Miss Creed, that I need to consult a jeweller."

"You, my lord? But it's my grandmother's tiger?"

"I can hardly let you lug a tiger skin about town and see you taken advantage of my dear. Especially as I think there may be a fortune in those eyes."

Lucilla's own eyes held a sparkle of hope as she raised them past the square jaw to the steady gaze, now quite close to hers.

"You think this may indeed be valuable? You think I may be able to leave the school?" Lucilla had been unable to imagine another future. It would take her years on a lowly teacher's income to save enough money to make it possible to leave otherwise.

Hugh laid aside the skin and grasped Lucilla's trembling hands in a warm and reassuring grip.

"Indeed, my dear, I very much hope that you will leave Miss Brodie's, even if the eyes do not turn out to contain emeralds and yellow diamonds. I don't like to see you wearing yourself out there."

Hugh gently kissed the knuckles of both her hands, sending shivers up to her throat.

"Come and let us discuss this over tea before I return you to the school."

Lucilla was hard put to remain standing. Her knees trembled as his lips touched her skin and his dark gaze looked longingly at her lips. Lucilla had never imagined Lord Marston taking such an interest in her. And then he thinks to discuss things over tea? What a maddening man.

ভাগ্য

Hugh arranged to collect Lucilla from the school the following afternoon and escort her to a reputable jeweller. He was surprised by the attraction he felt to the girl he had noted growing from gangly to, now he thought about it, perfectly graceful, over the years as she visited his mother. He knew her sad story, and had admired Lucilla's courage and control but never, until today, had he felt the tug of attraction. Lucilla was so untouched, so unsophisticated, compared to the usual society ladies he encountered. He needed to be careful with her.

ভাগ্য

As Hugh helped Lucilla into his curricle the next day, he reassured her that he had the tiger skin safely hidden in a portmanteau under their seat. As they drew up, the modest exterior of the jeweller's surprised Lucilla, but the designs displayed inside looked as expensive as they were tasteful.

"Lord Marston, welcome. Won't you come through?" The small precise man bowed to them both and guided them into another room, leaving an assistant at the counter. The jeweller was clearly expecting them. The groom had discreetly brought in the portmanteau and handed it over.

"Oh yes, I have seen these skins before." Mr Samuel took out a small magnifying glass and carefully examined the tiger's head and eyes, after Hugh placed the skin on a table. He pursed his lips. "But never with such beautiful jewels for the eyes. Such a rare colour in diamonds." Mr Samuel allowed himself a small smile.

Lucilla's gaze had been glued to the jeweller as he made his examination, holding her breath. She sighed and Mr Samuel focused on her for the first time.

"Quite a fortune you have here Lord Marston." Before Lucilla could correct the mistake, Hugh jumped in.

"What sort of value would you place on the stones, Samuel?"

Lucilla's jaw dropped at the thousands of pounds named.

"Naturally I would have to weigh them first, but I think that would be a conservative figure. Would you like me to go ahead?"

Hugh glanced briefly at Lucilla who starting to nod and again took charge of the transaction.

"At present, I just wanted to confirm my suspicions. I shall contact you if I decide to proceed."

"Naturally Lord Marston. Always a pleasure to be of service." Mr Samuel carefully restored the skin to the bag and bowed them courteously off the premises.

"Why didn't you let me speak to Mr Samuel?" Lucilla found her voice as soon as they were driving away. "You let him think they were yours." Lucilla was indignant at his lordship's assumption of proceedings.

"Calm those ruffled feathers Miss Creed, I was only trying to ensure your safety. If word of this got out and you were known to be the owner, your security at the school might be in jeopardy. I could never forgive myself if I had put you in danger." Concentrating on guiding his horses through the crowded thoroughfare, Hugh was unable to see Lucilla's indignant expression.

Lucilla had indeed puckered up at the hint of amusement in his first words, but when he alluded to danger her thoughts had sobered. An element of danger was the last thing Lucilla had expected in the upheaval of the week. The possibility of being independent, of being able to give up teaching, had pulled Lucilla out of the well of despondency over her grandmother's passing. Now Lord Marston was tensing her nerves with worry.

The curricle stopped, held up in the crush of traffic. A cry from Lucilla made Hugh turn towards her, only to see her leaping from her seat and dashing into the crowds.

"Stop thief!" Lucilla cried.

Just as Lord Marston had pulled the horses to a stop, an arm had reached into the carriage behind Lucilla's legs and pulled the portmanteau out. Shocked, she had launched herself from the vehicle and given chase. A small man in a grey coat was twisting his way through the crowds ahead of her, gripping the portmanteau.

Thrusting the reins into his groom's hands, Hugh jumped to the ground and followed her grey straw bonnet.

Lucilla's cries attracted the attention of a middle-aged gentleman, standing beside the road, just as the thief rushed past to a clearer alleyway. Using his walking stick the gentleman managed to trip the thief, who lost his grip on the portmanteau as he fell. Seeing Lucilla almost upon him, the thief judged his life worth more than the portmanteau and abandoned it as he ran off.

"Oh thank you sir. That was most helpful." Lucilla panted out as she stopped beside the portmanteau.

"I take it this is your property Miss?"

"Yes, indeed it is."

Lord Marston arrived as she said this.

"What were you thinking Miss Creed, dashing off after a thief? Wasn't I just warning you about dangers?" Hugh's heart had thumped painfully as he saw Lucilla jumping off the curricle. Now his fear was replaced by frustration. No fortune was worth his Miss Creed throwing herself into danger.

The gentleman who had stopped the thief clearly felt himself *de trop* and, saying "A pleasure to be of service Miss, my lord," bowed himself away.

Hugh was oblivious as he grasped Lucilla's arms, about to shake her, until she looked up at him, her chin jutting out in a stubborn gesture as she crossed her arms.

"Come, we'll discuss this back at the house." Swallowing his ire as the noise around him came back into focus, Hugh picked up the portmanteau, took Lucilla's elbow and pulled her back to the curricle.

⊂≋⊃

"Lord Marston." Lucilla had restrained herself until they were back in his mother's study.

"Please call me Hugh." His title grated, especially in Lucilla's irate tones.

"What do you mean?" She could not have heard aright. Much as she was coming to regard his lordship as a reliable friend, she felt that the social gulf between them could not be breached in this way.

"Miss Creed, Lucilla, I think our adventures have overcome such formality between us."

Hugh could hardly believe his own words as he tried to coax his name from this maddening young woman. But he couldn't ignore the sickening feeling of helplessness that had come over him as she had disappeared after the thief. He'd felt protective, a feeling so fierce that he'd surprised himself. Honesty compelled him to explore this new sensation.

No-one had really looked after Lucilla since her parents had left for India. Miss Brodie had been distantly kind and happy to have Lucilla fill a vacancy after her schooling finished, but having someone want to protect her was a new sensation. One she would like to rely on but didn't fully trust. She knew so little about men in general and one she had so lately looked up to as some sort of god was even more unfathomable.

"After all, I was ready to shake you like my annoying sister, in a public place." Not that Hugh thought of her in any way like a sister, but he wasn't yet ready to expose those feelings.

Feeling deflated, Lucilla sat down. Somehow a 'sister' was not how she felt.

"Well, what are we going to do about the thief then?" she huffed.

"Did you recognise him? I thought he might be Mr Samuel's assistant. I think I will send a note to a friend who is the local magistrate and see what he suggests." Hugh moved over to the desk to write and then dispatched the note with a footman and asked for some tea to be brought.

Hugh sat beside Lucilla and lifted her hand. At least she had said 'we'.

Fascinated by the warm, encompassing feel of his hand, Lucilla suppressed a shiver as she looked up into his intent eyes.

Hugh lost his train of thought and sat staring at Lucilla's questioning gaze, wondering what her lush lips and soft blond hair might feel like, until recalled to his senses by the rattle of the tea trolley. He stood hurriedly and moved to the window. Hugh tried to recall why he should keep his distance from this naïve young woman who was mourning her grandmother. It was getting more and more difficult.

Lucilla poured tea, her pulse humming through her body.

Before any discussion could resume, Lord River was ushered in. Medium height and slim, his energy nevertheless filled the room. After introductions, Hugh filled in the story for his friend.

"Well, Hugh, this is an interesting problem for us. Do you think the thief is likely to try again? If so, perhaps we should mount a guard here tonight. Yes, I think that's best." Without waiting for a reply, Lord River was off, saying he'd be back with reinforcements.

Timely though the interruption had been, Hugh still found

himself asking Lucilla if she would like to stay in the house with his mother for the night, unwilling to have her so far away as the school.

Quite dazed by the day's events, Lucilla agreed and wrote a note for Miss Brodie.

CR80

Laying her head, at last, on the pillows in the spacious room Lady Marston had shown her to that evening, Lucilla tried to study everything that had happened since hearing of her grandmother's passing. All that she was able to focus on, though, as she drifted to sleep, was the sight of her hand engulfed in a strong warm one and wondering what thoughts were behind a pair of mesmerising brown eyes.

CR80

Heartbeat pounding in her ears, Lucilla opened her eyes to darkness, wondering what had awakened her. Just as she started to make out the shadows in her room, she heard a scrape at her door. Lord Marston had insisted that she lock it, even with footmen watching the corridors and constables patrolling the grounds.

"Who is it?" Lucilla whispered. Then screamed as the door slowly opened, before a hand closed over her mouth, pulling her sideways.

"Where is it?" The words hissed in her ear as Lucilla struggled, her elbow thumping into the intruder's chest, her teeth closing on his hand. He yelped. She opened her mouth to scream again, just as pandemonium reigned.

Boots thundered into her room, the light from the hallway picking out the silhouettes of the men. Her attacker disappeared and Lucilla eased out of bed, anxiously pulling on her wrapper.

"I've got him." The triumphant shout came from beside Lucilla.

"She bit me!" Wailed the thief.

And then she was in Hugh's arms, crushed against his muscled chest.

"Are you alright love? Did he hurt you? Speak to me please." Hugh's raw pleas cut through Lucilla's surprise.

"Yes, yes, he didn't hurt me." Lucilla mumbled into his coat, before he eased her away from his chest, to see her face. Her laughing face. Laughing with relief.

"I'm f-fine." And then Hugh kissed her, drowning out the sounds around them.

"Oh God Lucilla, I'm never leaving you alone again." Hugh's heartbeat gradually slowed as he clutched his brave girl to his chest. His very own tigress, only to realise she was still laughing.

"What's so funny, my love?"

"I seem to have found more than my fortune in the tiger's eyes." Lucilla's smile lit up Hugh's heart.

"Yes, my dear, your very own tiger." Hugh said, grinning, before he pounced.

8

MORNING TRAIN

DIANNE INGLIS

The train trip to work was a lot more interesting since he had appeared. Ellaina wasn't sure where he was getting on... one stop before her... two? It didn't matter really. He was the main reason weekdays had suddenly become bearable, if only for the train ride to work and back each day.

She could never take it any further... talk to him or sit next to him even. What would she say?

"Hi there... nice shoes?" Yeek.

"Hi there... what are you reading?" Better... marginally.

She preferred the conversations she had with him in the sanctuary of her own mind. Where she was full of wit; smart and a little sassy. The conversations where actual words came out and her cheeks didn't flush the furious beetroot red they were wont to do. The ones where he gazed at her in awe with admiring eyes.

She knew what he was reading. He'd started on the Matthew Reilly series. Up to the second book.

Best keep the ogling surreptitious. She'd be mortified if he ever realised that she was eyeballing him. What was that expression? *Better to have someone assume you are a fool than to open your mouth and confirm it...*

∞

Ellaina nervously checked her reflection one last time before picking up her lipstick and sliding it into her bag. Her anticipation heightened as she walked from home toward the train station. Two big changes she'd made since he'd started catching the same train. Lipstick and skipping to the train with plenty of time to spare. No more running the last hundred metres and arriving with hair plastered to her forehead by the sweat of exertion and without a skerrick of make-up on.

Carriage number three. The quiet carriage. A deliberate choice because no-one on this carriage was interested in talking. They all came armed with a book, a laptop, the day's newspaper to focus on. There was no chance of a spontaneous conversation erupting that she'd have to respond to.

That had been her once, too. In her own world.

Now it meant she could look without being caught looking.

There he was. Usual seat. Facing her, three rows apart. She always sat in the same seat too, travelling forwards. She hated the sensation of the train going backwards and wondered why anyone chose to travel that way.

That shirt really made his blue eyes even bluer! And the tie he wore was almost the colour of her hair.

❦

James sat up a little straighter as the train pulled into the station. He had on his new blue shirt and red tie today. His hair was freshly cut and he'd tried some styling gel the barber had given him last night. It did tame his curly hair and made it sit a little neater. His brown shoes had an uncommon glean to them as well. Hell, the shoe shine guy was there for a reason, set up on the platform every morning, buffing shoes of the workers heading to town. James could almost see the reflection of his book in them, they were so polished.

He was in his usual seat, facing backwards. It had taken him weeks to overcome the feeling of freewheeling out of control with no visibility about where he was going. It was worth it though. At least this way he could watch the girl with the auburn hair.

Here she came. Head down, moving his way. She looked up as she stopped at her seat, her hand reached out to steady herself as the train moved off. Their eyes met for a nanosecond before he looked quickly down at his book.

New lipstick. He liked that shade of pink on her. It looked like she'd done something different to her hair too. He'd sneak another peak once she was reading her book. She'd been reading that one for a while now actually. Matthew Reilly. What a writer. He'd started reading these himself over the past few weeks.

❧❦☙

Ellaina could have sworn she'd seen blue eyes watching her as she stumbled, grabbing at the seat back to stop from making an absolute nong of herself. How mortifying if she'd fallen flat on her face! Probably thought she was a clumsy clot. She dared not look up again and concentrated on her book. Well she looked at the black ink on the page and turned one every once in a while.

❧❦☙

Yes, she'd *definitely* done something new to her hair. A bit shorter maybe, with a little flick up at the ends, softly curling around her face.

She was engrossed in her book this morning. A small frown puckered her brow as she turned pages at regular intervals. He'd love to talk to her but just wasn't quite game yet.

"What's the book you're reading?" would be the extent of his conversation skills.

❧❦☙

Ellaina hurried off the train and toward the escalator. Normally she hung back and waited until blue eyes got off. Then she could walk behind him, admiring the cut of his suit and the way the material stretched tautly across his shoulders.

But today she needed more help. Desperately.

Chimes sounded melodically as she pushed open the door to the little pop up store she'd first noticed about a week ago. Incense burned in a little elephant holder on the counter. Sandalwood, so calming. An array of dream catchers, statuettes, and crystals filled the room.

"Ah... my sweet. How lovely to see you again." A quirky gypsy character appeared from the back room. Strings of beads adorned her neck and a multi-coloured scarf encircled her hair.

The warmth exuding from her enveloped Ellaina, instantly putting her at ease.

"Good morning." Ellaina held her arms out, palms up imploringly. "I think... I think I might need... something *more*."

The woman nodded sagely as she moved around the counter to stand before Ellaina. Her beads clacked softly together as she walked.

"Did you try the oil on your pillow slip?" Ellaina nodded. "And the other things?"

"Yes. I've been doing *all* you suggested. I'm just not sure it's making any *difference* though. I still feel awkward and *klutzy*."

"This man you like... have you spoken to him yet?" Ellaina shook her head as she bit down on her lip.

"I still can't bring myself to. I doubt he even knows I exist. This morning he looked up as I walked his way, a cursory glance at best."

"Let me look at you..." The gypsy woman cocked her head to one side, examining her carefully, turning her one way then the other.

"You've restyled your hair. Excellent! It looks amazing my dear. So soft around your face. I *knew* it would become you."

"Do you think?" Ellaina reached up a self-conscious hand and tucked a strand behind her ear.

"Oh, I do my dear. I do. There is one thing though...."

"Yes?"

"If I may just say...?"

"Of course. I need all the help I can get!"

"You have a gorgeous little figure and yet you hide it beneath layers of heavy fabric." She tutted. "You're covered from head to toe."

Ellaina looked at herself in the mirror hanging from the wall. Black pants and jacket over a white blouse was her self-imposed uniform. So much easier to get ready each day. And to not draw any attention to herself.

"I'm not so sure..."

"Perhaps add a touch of colour... maybe a skirt instead of pants? If you've got them you may as well flaunt them, as they say..."

Did she 'have them'? Ellaina wasn't so sure.

⚜

James watched as she stood, her book tucked under her arm. She was in a hurry to leave the train this morning. By the time he reached the bottom of the escalator she was stepping off the top. Then she was out of sight. He would have to wait until tonight to see his russet-haired rose.

How he longed to talk to her. His brain froze and his heart

palpitated at the very thought! He had no choice but to recruit some more expertise to assist him.

The chimes above the door tinkled as he pushed it open.

"Ah ...good afternoon my dear. Welcome back."

"Good afternoon." James breathed in the scent of sandalwood and felt a calm descend over his body.

"Your new hair cut suits you very well!" The woman clapped her hands in delight. "And that red tie..."

"I'm sending subliminal messages as you suggested. Doesn't seem to be working though." James' shoulders slumped as he exhaled on a sigh.

"Now, now. Patience my friend, patience. Any progress at all?"

James shook his head, forlorn.

"Did you place the oil I gave you on your pillow last night?"

"Yes, I did. Slept like a log but still felt as awkward as ever this morning."

"This girl you like... did you see her today?"

James nodded, his mouth upturned slightly at the corners as her image came to mind.

"I don't think she even knows I exist." The faint smile faded.

"You might be surprised." The older woman reached forward and took him by the arm. "This girl... she is special, yes?"

"Oh, she really is. Hair the colour of a russet rose, eyes green like emeralds..." James felt the warm flush as blood coursed to his cheeks.

"And the gemstone? The one I gave you a few days ago? Have you carried it with you?"

James nodded, his hand instinctively snaking into his pocket, his fingers curling around the coolness of the stone as he withdrew it. It really did resemble a tiger's eye.

"This stone is powerful." The gypsy woman waved her finger before his face. "It will balance the yin and yang. You'll find courage to pursue your dream, to speak to your rose. What have you to lose, after all?"

What do I have to lose?

James stood taller. "Ok. I will... I'll do it. Tonight, I'm *going* to talk to her."

He hoped he didn't make a first-class fool of himself.

ᴄᴈ᭡ᴆᴐ

Ellaina hesitated momentarily before she pushed the heavy boutique door open. She normally avoided shopping for clothes, but today she was inspired by her new friend's encouragement and suggestions. So far, she'd been right about her hair style and lipstick.

"Can I help you?" Ellaina stepped into the store, letting the door swing closed behind her.

"I'm after a skirt please. Or perhaps a dress? Something bright... not black... maybe?"

When Ellaina left, she had a skip to her step. It had meant missing her usual train home. And seeing blue eyes. But wait until he saw her tomorrow!

She slipped her hand into one of the bags she carried - the fabric was soft and luxurious. She couldn't wait to get home and try it on again, with the new shoes in the other bag slung over her arm.

CঙৎৎৎৎC

James arrived at the station early, determination in his step. He was a man on a mission. He'd brushed his hair and applied just a smidge of his new gel, careful not to overdo it. He could feel the gemstone in his jacket pocket, reaching in every now and then to run his fingers over the smooth surface. Just knowing it was there settled the butterflies doing somersaults in his gut.

He couldn't see his russet-rose, though he carefully scoured the waiting crowds. Perhaps she was running late? *Unlikely.* She was always on time. Punctual, he liked that.

The train pulled in and he felt a sense of panic.

Where was she?

He made his way to his usual carriage and seat and sat. Waiting. Poised to move toward her and take the empty seat that was usually beside her. Determined to make his move. His fingers touched the stone.

Yes, he *could* do this.

The train pulled out of the station and her seat remained empty.

He sagged back against the seat. Did she stay away on purpose?

To avoid him?

Or worse... she'd found someone else. The make-up, the hairstyle. It made perfect sense.

He reached for the stone. He had to keep the faith.

Don't be stupid, he chided silently. Of course, that's not the reason. She'd simply missed this train.

He would see her tomorrow. He'd talk to her then.

∝∾

The dress was beautiful. Ellaina turned this way and that, watching her reflection as the soft green skirt swished back and forth before falling into perfect folds against her legs. She slipped on the new shoes and immediately felt *graceful*. And tall. So very different from her usual work attire, but this situation called for dramatic action.

Today she was going to speak to blue eyes.

∝∾

The train pulled into russet-rose's station. James craned forward peering along the length of the platform trying to pick her among the crowd of commuters.

The throng dispersed as people piled onto the train, leaving the platform empty.

There was no sign of her.

He scanned the platform desperately.

Nope.

As the train pulled away he slumped down into his seat.

Twice in a row now she'd failed to get on the train.

She was clearly avoiding him. How *could* he have been so *stupid*?

He pulled the stone from his pocket and weighed it in his hand. If the window had opened, he'd have heaved it outside. So much for the amazing powers of the tiger's eye.

What a load of bollocks.

CB80

"Crap, crap, crap." Ellaina knew she couldn't make it. These shoes, gorgeous they might be, were *not* made for running in.

The train's rear light disappeared round the bend beyond the station.

Taking blue eyes along with it.

CB80

The decision to catch the earlier train home was a no brainer. James couldn't bear thinking of the indifference he knew he would see on the face of the most beautiful girl he'd ever seen. The girl who had no interest in him, going out of her way to avoid him.

Minimise the pain.

That was the best strategy.

CB80

By the end of the day Ellaina's mood was dark. She'd been

late for work and her feet felt like hot coals on the ends of her legs. At least she'd get to see blue eyes soon. She quickened her step, determined to make it in plenty of time so she didn't appear flustered.

Was that blue eyes ahead of her on the platform? About to board the earlier train?

Surely not?

He was *always* on her train. Reliability. Such an important trait.

There was no doubting it. She'd recognise those shoulders anywhere. If he had *any* interest in her he'd *surely* wait for the train they always caught?

Don't be stupid, she chided silently.

The sensible thing would be to wait and see if things returned to normal in the morning. Probably a perfectly good explanation that didn't warrant jumping to crazy conclusions. Get a grip girl.

His seat remained agonisingly empty the next morning.

No further evidence required.

❧

James' mood got blacker as the day went on. *Pissed off* was a much better description. He'd been well and truly duped by the crazy old lady in the crystal shop. He had a good mind to tell her so and demand his money back.

❧

So much for good luck charms. Not to mention the rest! New

haircut, new dress, new shoes... with high heels for crying out loud.

Not. Happy. Jan.

CR80

The closer James got to the pop up shop the more determined he became. People shouldn't be allowed to manipulate gullible people... like him. The gypsy woman had picked him as a sucker that's for sure. He had even put oil on his pillowcase.

Oil that had probably left a stain to boot!

Grrr... that thought pushed him along faster.

The arcade was surprisingly quiet. He'd expected far more people out and about in their lunch break. Good thing. He'd be able to wrap up this business and get back to work.

The shop was closed. *Of course it was.*

Not only was it closed, steel bars barricaded the door and windows. As he drew closer, he could see that the shop was gone, vanished, disappeared. The shelves inside were empty, a lone envelope sat on the mat inside the door.

Charlatan! I knew it.

Fists clenched at his sides, he swung away, head down, chin tucked into the scarf around his neck.

And crashed headlong into someone coming the other way.

"Sorry... so sorry. All my fault. Should have watched where I was going." James grasped the arm of the poor person he'd nearly bowled over. She looked up, still teetering on one leg while her hand massaged a twisted ankle, stiletto shoe in her hand and wearing the most stunning green dress.

⚜

What a klutz! Why couldn't people watch where they were going instead of barrelling along and nearly bowling over innocent people? And falling from the height of her stupid new shoes had given her ankle a painful twist. Could nothing go well for her today?

Ellaina looked up, ready with her crossest scowl to show her displeasure. Her knees felt weak. She was suddenly glad of his hand on her arm as she gazed into eyes of the most amazing blue.

"It's you. From the train," she said.

"Yes."

"What are *you* doing here?"

James waved a hand at the shop.

"You came to this shop?"

He nodded. "It's gone, though."

"Darn it. I wanted to return something."

"Yes, me too." James pulled the tiger's eye from his pocket.

Ellaina reached slowly into her jacket pocket and withdrew her talisman of the past week. She opened her hand and heard his gasp.

"You too?"

She nodded, looking from the shop to him. Her mouth curved up into a smile.

"Yes, I was hoping this stone would give me the courage to talk to someone I liked," James said.

"Did it work?"

"I'm kind of hoping it did?" James slipped the tiger's eye back into his pocket. "Fancy a coffee?"

9

HOLD ME CLOSE

STELLA QUINN

October 1943
Prisoner of War Camp
Kanchanaburi, Thailand

*P*atch my love, we've just the one page and a beggarly one at that, and barely a moment in which to write. I've a pencil, still – as you'll see if this epistolary treasure defies my pessimism and reaches you – but there's a queue of lads lined up to borrow it, so I'd best be starting.

I'd tell you about me, here, in this hole that god's forgotten, but truth, Patch, it's all I see and all I smell, and I'm just about done with seeing it and smelling it.

Writing to you, though... I shut my eyes and imagine I'm with you. I'm in the chair with the crooked leg at the kitchen table, and the bread bin's winking at me from its home on the counter, there's your fussy little curtains, the yellow ones, with some fool flower on them I can never remember the name of... and you, Patch.

You know how I think of you? Not all gussied up in your tangerine lipstick and your dancing dress, with your Ma's pearls clipped on to your earlobes. That's how the world sees you. That's their Patch: pretty and powdered and me walking beside you proud as a man could be.

I see you different.

I see you at the table in the quiet of the morning. The little brown pot is steeping our tea, and the butcherbirds are fussing in the garden, wondering if they'll see a scrap of our toast.

And you in your dressing-gown. It's the blue one, with your initials stitched into the cloth above your heart. PJH: Mrs Patricia June Hogan. Makes me think of our wedding night, and what a bumbling wonderful mess of a night it was, my love.

Lola pressed a hand to her mouth, half laughed. "I can't believe I'm crying over a letter. I'm so pleased you found this."

Sam's voice was distorted through the microphone. These computer conferences were the pits. How she wished they could meet in person for once. "Read the next bit."

There's scones fresh from the oven, pumpkin ones because the vine down the backyard has gone berserk, and a great chunk of yellow butter bigger than a man's fist, and every time you pick up your tea cup, I hear the little clinking noise your ring makes on the china handle.

Lola hauled in a breath. The ring! This was the first mention of it, after all the hours of searching she and Sam had put in.

She looked up from the printed copy of the old letter in her hand and shot a smile at Sam, whose face grinned at her from the pixelated corner of her screen. She dragged her eyes away from his deep grey ones and returned to the last of the hastily scrawled words.

> *I think of that sound when the night's at its blackest here in the camp, Patch, and fear's got me gripped like a python on a rat. Your ring, and its little yellow stone with some fool name I can never remember either. I shut my eyes, and I hold that memory close.*
>
> *Do me a favour, will you, love? Hold the ring close to your heart and I'll know I'm not really here, in this hellhole, closer to death every day, but with you, where I most want to be.*
>
> *Hold me close, Patch*
>
> *Love, Bill.*

Lola dropped the letter and grabbed a tissue to mop her streaming eyes.

"Now I'm having a mascara crisis, Sam," she said. "I can't believe you found that letter. Where? How?"

"Remember that research you did for me on the Hogan family tree?"

"Of course, yes. But I don't recall anything about a letter."

Sam gave a grin, cocky as hell despite the thousand

kilometres of internet cable that separated them. "You librarians don't get to have all the fun, Lola. I had a hunch, drove damn near six hours to follow it, and that letter was my reward."

"Tell me everything."

"I will, but—"

Sam's grin became a little less sure.

"What? What is it?"

He looked awkward, then rushed in to speech. "I hope it's not against the rules or anything – but I'm coming to Brisbane. I wondered if we could, um—"

Lola forgot to breathe, she just rushed straight into the gap of sound, not caring if it was Sam's hesitation or the vagaries of high-speed internet cable that had caused it. "Meet up? You and me?"

He shrugged. "Yeah. If you'd like."

Holy cow, yes, she would like. "Sure," she said, clearing her throat so the words came out calmly, rather than in a lather of excitement. "Let's meet up."

"Okay then."

"Okay then." She could feel her cheeks flushing and decided the prudent course of action would be to get herself off this skype call to regroup. To think. To remember not to gush like a raging ninny-hammer just because the man she'd had a crush on for eight long lonely months was finally, *finally*, coming to town.

"Gotta go," she said, and clicked the *End Call* button with one quick tap of her finger on the mouse.

CЗΘ

"Tell. Me. Everything."

Lola took a sip of her friend Vicki's water and grinned. The riverbank below the State Library had trapped the midwinter sunlight, and the two of them sat on the warm grass, their backs to the broad trunk of a melaleuca.

"We've only got an hour for lunch. I'm not sure I can condense the woeful history of my love life and today's skype bombshell into a sixty-minute story."

Vicki ripped the tab from a tuna tin and dumped its contents into her salad. "Let me condense it for you. Chapter one: bitter breakup so long ago even you are struggling to remember the lowlife's name. Chapter two: lonely days and lonely nights ensue. Chapter three: genealogy research job comes into the library and you become wholly engrossed in the backstory of a grazier from outback Queensland who's wondering why he's just inherited a tiger's eye ring wrapped in a small silk Japanese flag. How am I doing so far?"

Lola picked a crumb from her tartan tights and tossed it to the ibis who was displaying a beady-eyed interest in her lunch. "Sam Hogan, research query number 36HJ-1, Hogan family tree," she said, drawing the words out in a long, blissful sigh.

Her friend gave her a nudge and spoke through a mouthful of salad. "Just cut to chapter four for me: the skype bombshell."

"Okay." Bombs away. "Sam's coming to Brisbane. He wants to meet."

"Yowza, that *is* news. When you say meet, do you mean in a reference room so you can pore over dusty records? Or meet as in..." she waggled her eyebrows and dropped her voice to a jungle panther purr, "... *meet?*"

Lola rubbed her hand through her thatch of dark hair. "I wish I knew."

"This is so exciting. Who'd have thought a reference librarian would score a hot date at work?" Vicki reached down and flicked a green ant off her shoe. "Jokes aside, Lola – Sam may not turn out to be the hero you've been daydreaming about."

She crossed her fingers where Vicki couldn't see them. "I know that."

Her friend made a sceptical noise loud enough to scare the ibis into flight. "Lola. You've a soft heart and a romantic disposition, which is why you're always crying in the archive room. Prepare yourself for disappointment, that's all I'm saying."

CRBO

But when Lola set eyes on Sam Hogan, grazier and amateur genealogy sleuth, six days and four hours later, she wasn't disappointed at all.

At all.

Dark hair curling over his ears... deep grey eyes, thickly lashed... a tan that spoke of long hours outdoors... she let out a long and shaky breath.

Did he ride a horse, she wondered? Heavens above, she hoped so, because a mental vision of him flashed across her brain: Sam, riding a stallion in slow motion across a windswept wheat field, the sun setting over distant mountain ranges, his shirt recklessly agape at the neck, his strong thighs gripping the heaving beast beneath him—

Woah there, Lola.

She frowned. She was a librarian, damn it. She shelved her books in the fact section, not the lust-in-the-dust section.

His finger dinged the bell on the unattended queries counter, and she rose from her seat behind the glass office wall.

"Go boldly, Lola," she whispered, then walked out to meet him in the flesh.

CRBO

Oh. The doe-eyed librarian who had been his online friend

for months now was *short*. She stood before him, a smile on her face, and he grinned, because he couldn't damn well help it, he was so happy to be here, in person, at long bloody last. Her face he knew: he could have shut his eyes and described it to every single one of the thirty-six people who lived within a hundred-kilometre radius of his cattle station. Dimples. A fondness for mascara and dangly ear rings of every shape and colour. A forehead that puckered when she was concentrating, a smile that wavered when she read something sad.

She was dressed in black: black tights, black boots, black skivvy that clung in all sorts of ways that he was keen to check out but steeled himself not to. And around her neck she'd wrapped some thin sort of scarf the colour of Simpson Desert sand.

"Hey," she said.

That voice. Low, warm, sweet. He could have fallen in love with her for that voice alone some nights, in the quiet of his homestead with just the dog and his research project for company, and Lola calling him with snippets of information, then chatting awhile. She'd filled in so many blanks in his life, not all of them with research. She was the one who'd told him the stone in his ring was tiger's eye, and supposedly gave people courage to make tough decisions; that the flag it had been wrapped in was a *yosegaki hinomaru*, a Japanese good luck flag given to a soldier to carry into battle.

She'd snuck in bits of her life, too; enough to have him hoping that he wasn't the only one finding an online relationship nowhere near enough.

He had the old ring in his pocket, so he decided it was now or never to put its courage building properties to the test. No way was he going to say hello like some random stranger. Only, he was going to have to bend a little to say hello the way he wanted to, because he hadn't expected her to be quite so little.

"Hey, Lola," he said, grinning. "You are such a short-arse."

She raised her eyebrows, but he didn't give her a chance to say hello, he leaned down and wrapped his arms around her, spun her in a tight grip while he hugged her good and proper. She smelt like sunshine and lavender fields, and after a second's surprise she softened in his arms, hugged him back.

He set her back on her feet, watched with interest the colour flooding her cheeks. "I'm here," he said. Needlessly, but the fact seemed important. He wanted to shout it out so the whole library would hear.

She grinned. "I was thinking this would be awkward. I guess not."

"You want to grab a drink?"

"Let me grab my coat."

෴

Lola hurried into her office. It wasn't quite five, and she hadn't officially finished work, but if ever there'd been a time to not let a paltry issue like a few minutes get in her way, that time was now.

She shot a quick text off to Vicki as she grabbed her coat and bag.

Having drinks with Sam. Not sure where. Fingers crossed. No disappointment yet... #manbliss

Understatement of the year. She'd nearly swooned when he picked her up and swung her around. She pressed a hand to her still-thudding heart, then flicked off the office lights, glanced one last time at her phone as it beeped in her hand.

Be sensible. And if you're not sensible, be prepared to share every detail with me tomorrow. Every. Detail. Love Vx

She slid the phone into her bag and took a calming breath.

ᎶᏁᎶ

Lola led Sam through the busy quadrangle below the State Library, across the busier road, and over to the bar in Fish Lane, which was fashioned from dilapidated shipping containers held together by trendiness and graffiti. She snagged a table, waited until a waiter had plonked two glasses of shiraz in front of them.

She took a sip, shy suddenly. "So," she said. Talking in person *was* different; there was so much more to be aware of. Sam's body language: relaxed, confident, flirty even. She wasn't used to flirty guys paying her attention. Sam's smell: road dust and clean linen and some unnameable man-smell that made her want to roar, just a little, down deep in her throat. And the rest of him: all six foot of healthy, sun-kissed male. Words failed her.

"You're not asking me how I found the letter," Sam said, reaching forward, and clinking his glass to hers.

She clinked back, and just like that the noise cut through the imbalance she'd been feeling ever since Real Sam took over from Virtual Sam. The clink of glass on glass – the clink of wedding ring on tea cup – of course she wanted to hear about the letter.

"Tell me everything."

"Yep." Sam reached into his satchel and pulled out an envelope. On top was taped the family tree she'd taught him to populate from public records. Marriage registries, public service records, birth certificates... all jigsaw pieces that could be found a home once you knew how.

"The ring and the flag that we've been studying came to me when my mother died, but I was wrong to assume they were from her side of the family. My father died when I was little and I was raised by my stepfather, Wally Kidd. The Hogan family wasn't talked about much, but I did remember my mother telling me the Hogans came from Goondiwindi. I started looking around for any descendants who might still be in the district."

"And?"

"I found some cousins, went to see them. As soon as I mentioned the flag and the ring, they were able to fill me in."

Lola sat back in her chair. "I can't believe we didn't twig to this earlier. What did they tell you?"

"My new cousin Anne had Bill's war record. His real name was William Hogan. I've got it here, you'd better read it."

She held the page to the candle. *William L Hogan... taken prisoner March 1942, believed died of disease Burma 1944 location unknown.*

The poor man. And Patch! Waiting all that time, holding a little ring close to her heart. "So he never came home."

"No. And Patch, or Patricia as she was known to Anne, remarried, but stayed in touch with the Hogans. When she remarried, she returned Bill's ring to his mother, which was how it somehow filtered down to me."

A mystery solved. But as so often happened when you researched the past, the endings could be bittersweet.

Sam's hand squeezed hers. "Why the sad face?"

She shrugged. "Oh, the war. So many lives destroyed."

"Mmm. I've been thinking of going there, you know. To Thailand. There's a war cemetery. I'd like to know where Bill was buried... if he was buried. Might take a bit of research, Lola."

"Was that a proposition?"

Sam cleared his throat. "Just thinking out loud. But speaking of propositions. I was wondering if you fancied taking a little road trip out west. I've internet out there, in case you did want to help me dig around a little more into Bill's past. I know it's a big ask."

It was a huge ask! My god, could she? *Should* she?

"I've got loads of leave owing," she said, more to herself than to him, then blushed. She wanted to say yes, but how well did she really know Sam after all?

He signalled the waiter, handed a few notes over to pay for their drinks. 'Shall we find somewhere to have dinner??"

She nodded. "I'd like that."

ℭℜℬ

"About that visit ..."

Lola paused from scrabbling in her handbag for her keys. Sam had driven her home in his dusty Landcruiser after hours of wandering and stargazing by the river. "I have to think about it, Sam."

Who was she kidding? She'd not been thinking about anything else since the second he'd suggested it.

"I've got something with me that might help you make your decision."

She cocked her head. "Oh?"

He reached into the pocket of his jeans, pulled out a length of chain that glittered in the light spilling from the interior of his car. On it, spinning like a compass, was a thin gold ring with a small yellow stone.

"Oh my god, you brought it with you!"

Patch and Bill's ring. She held up her fingers to touch it, felt Sam's fingers close around hers so the ring sat tight within the curl of their joined hands.

She looked up as he looked down, his dark eyes fixed on hers. He moved, just a little... as she did. He smiled, just a little... as she did. A whisper separated them, then a breath, then a heartbeat. His lips touched hers and he brought his hand in close, so the ring they clasped rested against her heart.

He moved then, and his mouth was soft as a promise, warm as a gift. "Make the brave choice, Lola," he whispered. "Come and visit."

And as she watched his tail lights merge into the stream of traffic, she already knew she'd be saying yes.

10

SECOND CHANCE AT LOVE

FIONA GREENE

R aine Cooke watched until the parade disappeared down Main Street, then turned her back on the crowd, hundreds of people decked out in a sea of bright outfits. She wandered to the edge of the park and breathed in the peace and solitude of the view over the lush, rolling foothills to Mount Warning.

She tried to ignore her mounting unease.

"How are you holding up?"

Raine's breath left her chest in a whoosh.

Bryson Stevens.

She'd know that deep timbre anywhere.

Raine flicked another quick glance at the mountain.

At her escape.

She straightened her shoulders and tried to summon a smile.

"Bryson, I didn't know you were here."

"Clearly," Bryson paused, "You're still here." Pain sliced through her. She didn't trust her voice not to waver. So she stayed silent. "This has to stop." His tone was conversational.

"This, what?"

"This thing we've got going where if I drive into town, sure as eggs, you drive out the other side." He stood beside her, staring at the mountain. "The urban myth around here is that we're actually the same person because, for the last three years, no-one's ever seen us in the same town, let alone the same street."

Raine considered mounting a defence, but he was right. God knows, ever since she'd come back to town, she'd planned her days with military precision, so their paths wouldn't cross. "I thought it was best." She raised her gaze to meet his.

And her heart stopped.

Those eyes.

She remembered them as blue.

But not slate blue.

The silky shirt that clung to the broad expanse of his shoulders was the same vibrant hue, the fabric shot with grey, silver, and turquoise. It threw flashes of peacock as he moved, reminding her of the blue tiger's eye she'd been redesigning this week.

A gorgeous stone in an antique setting that Bryson had given her for Christmas. Until a month ago, it had languished in a box, unworn and unloved. Now, she was ready to liberate its beauty through redesign. Projects like that were the highlight of her jewellery business.

"Earth to Raine-y." Was it his use of her nickname, or his

shoulder brushing hers, that sent a shiver up her spine?

No, it was lust, pure and simple.

The shirt was gorgeous, but his eyes were mesmerising.

Breath-taking.

She couldn't look away.

Heat flooded up her face. She searched for something to say and blurted the first thing that came to mind. "I like your shirt."

Bryson tilted his head and stared at her. "Thanks." He cleared his throat. "Your dress is… very tropical."

"Tropical?"

"Leafy. Overgrown. It's got so much foliage the farmer in me wants to say it's in need of herbicide."

"Gee, thanks. I see you haven't been spending your time at charm school."

Bryson looked her up and down and Raine's heart rate bumped up a notch. "I was joking. You're as beautiful as I remember."

"Thank you. Your cousin designed this dress."

"Lara?"

Raine nodded. "Yeah. She's one of my best friends."

He gestured to his sleeve. "She's great, isn't she? I didn't own anything bright, but when I rang her, she rescued me. I owe her."

Raine's eyes prickled with tears.

The entire town had turned out in bright colours for a parade to honour the life of Georgina McElroy, the town's matriarch, who was turning one hundred. A woman who'd always had time for her, no matter what. People who lived for their community like old Georgie Mac were why she'd made her home in Cullgen Creek.

The murmur of voices grew louder as the crowd dispersed and Raine's stomach knotted.

She shouldn't be talking to Bryson.

The last thing she wanted was for the gossip to start.

Again.

Raine Cooke. Homewrecker.

The conversations grew louder and the skin between her shoulder blades burned. She didn't turn, instead, she focused on the towering remnants of the ancient volcano, the only thing still visible through the blur of tears.

The clack of heels stopped behind her.

So did the chatter.

"Lock up the husbands." The falsetto was all innocence. "The homewrecker's in town."

"No." The whispered plea escaped before she could stop it. Raine braced herself.

"Damn right, no," Bryson muttered under his breath. He clamped an arm around her waist and spun the two of them around. "Ladies."

There was a chorus of "Hello Bryson."

Raine couldn't speak. Hell, if not for Bryson's muscular forearm, she probably wouldn't still be standing.

The arm around her waist cinched tighter, so close she could feel the heat of his body. "You all know my good friend, Raine?"

Of course, they knew her. They'd known her most of her life.

The women remained silent.

Raine abandoned her study of the pavement and risked a peek at Bryson's face.

His eyes had turned to steel, all light in them gone.

Raine's heart shattered into a thousand pieces.

She'd seen that look before.

She'd been the one to cause it, the day she broke it off with Bryson.

It seemed like yesterday they'd spent that explosive summer together, totally absorbed in one another. She'd left home to take up her jewellery apprenticeship in the city. He'd turned up out of the blue. She'd been young and impetuous, and she'd thought she was in love. Bryson was older, reckless and, as she found out come autumn, married, and separated from a local girl.

Well, happily married if you listened to what his ex and her country club mates had to say.

No longer happily married if you listened to Bryson.

And she hadn't listened to Bryson.

More fool her.

Better a fool than a coward.

Raine straightened and lifted her eyes.

The women glared back.

"Still?" He glared at each of the women in turn. "No more, ladies. This ends here. This ends now."

The air crackled.

Then, without saying a word, the women turned their backs and walked away.

"Raine, I'm so sorry."

Raine blinked furiously. She didn't want the tears burning her eyes to land on Bryson's gorgeous new shirt.

Bryson hauled her against his chest and with one strong hand, laid her head against his shoulder. He ran a gentle hand over her hair and whispered, "It's okay, now."

She lost the battle.

A big fat tear escaped.

Then a second.

As the dam burst, she sobbed for all she was worth in the sanctuary of his arms.

And he let her.

He held her tight, the way he always had, and let her cry.

⚜

The slam of car doors and hum of engines gradually died, replaced by the rustle of the gum trees and the harsh calls of the crows. The guest of honour for the parade was long gone, but still, they stood at the edge of the park.

One second Raine was deep within her misery, swallowing down on a shuddery sob, the next she was breathing in citrus and spice and sandalwood, and staring at the damp patch spreading across Bryson's chest. Under her cheek, his heartbeat loud and strong.

Memories washed over her. It was three long years since the

last time she'd been crushed up against Bryson's chest, breathing in the gorgeous scent of him.

Reality came crashing back with a vengeance.

Great.

First contact with the man she'd loved all those years ago, and she'd made a complete fool of herself, blubbering all over his shirt. Heat flooded up from her neckline. Next time they were about to cross paths, it would be Bryson Stevens making the beeline out of town.

Raine didn't want to move, but she knew she had to. If she left now, the country club set might spare Bryson from their venom. She straightened her shoulders and lifted her head, then willed every ounce of strength still in her body into her arms and pushed on Bryson's chest.

"Not so fast." Worry was etched into Bryson's face. He shook his head and tried to speak, then stopped.

Raine looked up at Bryson and nodded. "It's okay. One day, they'll get sick of it. Move on."

His look was incredulous. "It's not okay," His voice rose as he spoke, "It wasn't okay back then, and it's not okay now. What are they thinking? They're grown women."

"Your ex was their friend. Remember?"

"My ex didn't know how to be a true friend," Bryson spoke through gritted teeth. "She was using them, the same as she used everyone."

"They considered her a friend, and their loyalties still lie with her. I wish I had friends half that loyal," she paused, "That's why I'm not angry. Not anymore."

Bryson's eyes were steely again. "It was over with the ex, long before anything happened between us."

"I know." Deep in her heart, she did know it. "I'll never forgive myself for not believing you back then. Some days, I think I should do what she did; leave town, start afresh. I'm sorry for the way I treated you. I'm sorry I didn't believe you."

The words she'd wanted to say for such a long time hung in the air between them.

"I understand," Bryson cleared his throat.

"We were both caught up in a malicious lie," he paused, "I wondered why you returned."

Because leaving meant I'd never see you again, not even from a carefully orchestrated distance.

Raine buried that thought. "My dream was to re-open grandpa's business and nobody, not even those women, was going to stop me." She straightened her shoulders again. "You and I did nothing wrong."

"I hate that this is still happening. The people of Cullgen Creek should be above this."

"Ninety-nine percent of them are. The other one percent..." Raine trailed off.

"Let's get out of here." Bryson took her hand and they walked towards his sports utility and her hatch, now the only cars left in the angle parks that bordered the park.

Raine stopped. "I'm not going to the hall." It wasn't just the other women. She'd spent three years dreaming about Bryson, desperate to call him, or drop over, but not letting herself act. She had to get away before she did something stupid.

Bryson rubbed his thumb over the back of her hand. "No, me either." He walked her over to her car. "I couldn't guarantee I wouldn't say something. I don't want to ruin Georgie Mac's day."

Raine faced him and placed her finger across his lips. "Don't say anything, please. It makes them worse."

"You should go to the police."

Raine's smile was bittersweet. "You know, there's no law against being nasty."

"There should be."

"I know." She felt in her purse for her keys. "I should go." Just as she'd decided to rework the tiger's eye from a beautiful reminder of past pain to something that bought her joy, she had to move on. Saying goodbye to Bryson, that was one Band-Aid she wanted to rip off quickly. "Thanks for today." Before she could overthink it, she stood on tiptoe and feathered a kiss onto his cheek. "Sorry about your shirt."

ভিত্তি

Bryson stared at Raine, gorgeous in her leafy green dress, stunned by how quickly she'd tried to slip away. "Wait." He grabbed hold of her car door before Raine could close it "Let's get a coffee."

Raine stilled.

Froze, more like it.

"Is that a good idea?" She didn't look at him, instead, she stared straight ahead, her knuckles white on the steering wheel.

"Why not? We know where everyone who makes your life hell is right now. We need to steer clear of the hall, but we should have the rest of the town to ourselves."

Raine gnawed on her lip. "Maybe the roadhouse?"

"We should go downtown. Sit in plain sight. See what happens?"

"No."

His heart shattered at her swift refusal. It wasn't okay to hurt Raine. She'd done nothing wrong.

Guilt burned like acid in his mouth. He should have done something about the rumours when he first heard them. He should have checked on Raine. But she'd said she wanted space.

"I really have to get going."

She was still trying to escape.

Think fast.

Raine had made him feel alive that summer, and he hadn't felt like that since. He couldn't let her go again. "I'm looking at a block of land, up near the national park. We could grab a coffee and drive up there. I'd love your opinion."

"Really?" Her tone suggested she thought he was making it up.

"Yes, really. It's listed with Bonds if you want to check it out. The website has photos of an ocean view," he chuckled, "I'm pretty sure they took the shot from a drone."

He watched Raine struggle with her decision. She wanted to come. He could see it. But if she did, she'd face consequences.

Anger at her tormentors raged through him.

That indecision and fear, so obvious on her face, had probably played out thousands of times.

Not anymore.

"It's closer to Suffolk than Cullgen Creek. It might be the one," he paused, "I'd really like it if you came and looked."

Raine stared at him, then looked down the Main Street towards the hall. Finally, she spoke. "I'd like that too."

"Great."

Raine stuck her key in the ignition.

"I can give you a lift." Now that they were together, he didn't want to let her out of his sight. Just in case he never caught up with her again.

Raine bit her lip. "Do you think my car will be okay here?"

"Yeah, it'll be fine. Everyone's at the hall." He hoped he was right.

After a few seconds Raine pulled the key from the ignition.

"Thanks, I'll come with you."

Bryson's heart lifted. "Let's go".

"Oh," Raine breathed, "I'm in love with your block of land already."

Bryson had pulled off the road in front of the for-sale sign. "It's the old Potter place. Forty acres. Plenty big enough for a few horses and cattle."

Raine gazed around, trying to get her bearings.

"That's east." Bryson pointed across the road to a block with a forest of trees crowding the fence line.

"I'm not seeing ocean views," Raine laughed, "Maybe from the top of that tree there?"

"I'd have to build a treehouse," he laughed, "Come on, grab your coffee and we'll have a look."

Raine stared down at the sensible pumps on her feet. "Um, I didn't really think this through. These aren't walking shoes."

"No, they aren't," he thought for a second, "Hang on."

Bryson dived behind the seats and pulled out a blanket and a couple of cushions. "We don't have to walk, we can sit in the tray and try to get a feel for the place from here."

"That'd work." She kicked off the pumps, then once she was sure Bryson wasn't looking, her stockings, so impractical for summer in Australia, joined the shoes in the foot well.

Oh, the freedom.

Raine stopped. What was happening to her?

For years, she'd maintained an image of decorum, designed to blend in, and now she was about to sit barefoot in the back of a utility, with the man who she'd loved more than life itself, and she was going to do it on the side of the road where anyone could see.

The sort of behaviours she'd avoided all these years because they could be construed as 'wrong'.

But the sorts of things her heart knew were so right.

Bryson was waiting for her at the tailgate. He held out his hand and even the touch of his fingers as he helped her up into the tray made her insides turn to mush.

Seconds later they were sitting shoulder to shoulder, thigh to thigh against the back of the cab.

"This is fabulous Bryson."

"It's pretty special," he paused, "Close enough to Cullgen Creek, but far enough away for some distance."

"Sounds perfect," Raine laughed, "But it isn't me you have to convince."

"It could be you." Bryson's words were so soft she almost missed them. He faced her and the intensity in his eyes sent shivers down her spine. He took a huge breath. "I know we've been apart for a long time, but everything I've done since we split, every decision, there's been a voice in my head saying, 'what would Raine think?'. When I saw you today, my heart knew. My head knew. I want you back in my life." He leaned forward and brushed the lightest of kisses on her lips.

Tears blurred her vision.

Her heart soared, then plummeted. Bryson's words would be perfect, bar one little thing. "You saw what happened today." Her heart started to pound. "I couldn't put you through that," she paused, "I wouldn't."

"You aren't putting anyone through anything. And neither are they. I won't put up with it. They won't mess with you anymore," he paused.

"Won't mess with us," he corrected.

Raine's stomach churned. She didn't want Bryson to fight her battles, but maybe, just maybe, having him with her might give her the courage she needed to fight them herself.

Did she dare believe him?

Raine closed her eyes.

She was ready to move on, and she wanted Bryson to be a

part of that. Any doubts she'd had about redesigning the Tiger's eye he'd gifted her disappeared. She'd make it into a piece that celebrated their future, and she'd wear it with pride.

With love.

Her eyes flicked open. "You and me," she whispered, her heart pounding. She put her hand on his chest and touched her lips to his. "Sounds pretty good to me."

He laughed, took her hand and kissed each of her fingers. "Together."

"Together," Raine agreed, her heart soaring, "The way it always should have been."

11

TYGER, TYGER

FIONA MARSDEN

*T*yger, Tyger, Burning Bright.

Margaret Delancourt had never seen a tiger, but she was convinced that Lord Ainsley West was almost certainly the human embodiment of such an animal.

Sleek and powerful, dusky locks flopping over his handsome face, he prowled rather than walked across the ballroom. The cause of many a maidenly flutter. But Margo guarded her heart, which remained achy and sore after her last encounter with Lord West in Paris, at the time of Napoleon's incarceration on Elba. Almost a full year had passed since that momentous time.

She might be fond of the exotic beast of Blake's poem, which she had learned as a child, but Ainsley West was not a man to become fond of if you wished to remain heart whole. His fascination lured the unwary, his eyes speaking worlds of excitement and challenge; but he remained untamed.

"Miss Delancourt." He bowed low, his thick black lashes concealing the feral brightness of his tiger-eyes. She braced herself for the spark of amber as he met her gaze. "May I have this dance?"

A waltz. It had only been fashionable in London this past few seasons, so she had never chanced to dance it with Lord West. In her first season only the daring would stand up for a waltz at a private party. Ainsley West had been there for her come-out. Had raised hopes that had been dashed when he'd left London halfway through the season. It had been two years before he emerged from wherever he'd been to join the celebrations in the French capital.

Her aunt had been too strict a chaperone to allow her to waltz during the brief sojourn in Paris, before the escape of the Corsican monster had sent them scuttling back home.

Aware of the curious stares of her fellow wallflowers, Margo reluctantly placed her hand in the outstretched one. Even through the gloves, heat flowed. His hand at her waist sent a sear of flame to jolt the ice in her chest. She closed her eyes to block out the lick of fire in his eyes.

Tyger, Tyger, Burning Bright.

"You dance well, Margo."

Her eyes flicked open, but she kept them fixed on the intricacies of his neckcloth, intrigued by a glimpse of a pin almost hidden in the folds. She blinked away the pain of a half-forgotten memory and looked past him to the other dancers whirling around the room. "It is not for want of practice. I have been out for over three years now."

"Three years. Practically an ape leader."

"This will be the last season. My father has commanded me to return home to make way for Cicely."

He stumbled but recovered. "My God, is Cissy ready to make her come-out?"

"She is turned eighteen. There was talk of her coming to London last season, but Papa had hopes of bringing Seldon up to scratch for me."

His grip tightened almost painfully on her hand. "You and Seldon? Not a match I would consider for my daughter."

"He married Maria Althorne."

"Poor Maria. Poor Margo." His drawl deepened to a syrupy consistency. "You don't have much luck with your suitors."

"I am content. The country suits me." She dared a glance up at his face, taking in the tightness of his jaw and the grim line of his beautiful mouth. "I suppose you will be taking your bride home to Mallings for the summer."

He halted the dance, halfway through a turn, leaving her dizzy. "My bride?"

"Lady Gabriella. I was informed you married her in Paris and have spent the next months on your bridal tour. Did you go to Italy? Was it as beautiful as they say?" It hurt to keep the buoyant tone in her voice, but Margo felt she had done a creditable job. Even if her throat ached and her eyes stung. She was conscious of the glares of the other couples as they swirled around the motionless pair in the centre of the ballroom.

Lord West swung her into motion again but this time she could tell he had a definite destination in mind, ducking and weaving between the gyrations of their fellow dancers.

The wide doors onto the paved area that led to the gardens

were open to the unusually warm spring night. Margo stumbled as he hurried her down the broad stone steps. His arm tightened at her waist, bringing her hard against his side. Her breath caught at the solid strength of him.

Memory clouded her senses and she allowed him to guide her deeper into the shrubberies. They emerged at a secluded gazebo, overlooking a pool that shone dark and serene in the dappled moonlight coming through the trees.

In the forests of the night.

"You know the discreet hiding places all too well, I fear."

He snorted, releasing her and moving a little away. "Lady Appleby is my Godmother. I grew up playing hide and seek in these grounds."

"I had forgotten."

"You prefer to think ill of me, Margo?"

Heat coloured her cheeks. "No, no, of course not."

Even in the shadowy red tinged light of the gazebo, tastefully lit by a ruby glass lantern, she could see the sneer that marred his mouth and drew harsh lines from nose to jaw. He had aged, these last years. She had noticed it in the ballroom but had had little time to study him in the movement of the waltz.

Still beautiful. Still with that air of danger. But the spark in those savage eyes masked a weariness he was at pains to hide with his heavy-lidded gaze. It seemed these years had been hard also for him.

❧

Ainsley folded his arms across his chest and scrutinized

Margaret Delancourt's flushed face. Her soft brown hair was pulled up to a topknot of ringlets, and wispy curls framed her heart shaped face with its neat nose and determined mouth and chin. Her blue eyes were wary as they evaded his, her skin flushed with the glow of the lamp. Little had changed in the year since she'd returned to London and he'd travelled in the opposite direction. Few would have recognised him in those weary weeks after infiltrating the vanguard of Napoleon's army.

He had thought to be freed in the immediate aftermath of Waterloo, but the commander in chief himself had insisted Ainsley travel to Vienna and Russia, to sound out the political situation with the allies. Now at last he could take up his own life.

"I am not married, Margo."

"Not?" Her hand clutched at the stone at her throat. Interesting that she still wore it, believing as she did in his betrayal.

"The widow and I had dealings in a matter of business. But no more than business."

"I was certain. Surely, I could not be mistaken. More than one of our acquaintance insisted it were true."

Once again, Ainsley rued the exigencies of his past calling. It had suited his superiors at the time to allow the rumours full sway. At least Margo had not heard, or perhaps given credence to, the ones that held Gabby to be his mistress. The rumours protected both of them, though he and Gabby had parted ways almost immediately.

"The rumour mill was active, with the hurried removal of the English from Paris and information was likely scrambled."

Her pale forehead creased. "But surely you did not return to London. I should have heard. And Lady Preston most certainly did not."

"You forget that she is French. I must assume that she had her own reasons for not returning."

That seemed to give her pause. "She has family in France?"

"I don't know. Neither do I care. I have no interest in her at this moment. It is you I wish to converse with, Margo."

She stiffened then, looking around at the secluded space. "We have nothing to say. Pray return me to the ballroom." Her voice, usually so soft and tender, had the chill of a Moscow winter.

"Even though you know that I have not dallied with another."

A small dimple flashed out as her mouth curled and then compressed under force of will. "You sound like a demi-beau."

"Do I look like one too?" He felt odd, back in formal clothes after the long months of tattered uniforms and other less comfortable raiment.

Her eyes narrowed. "You look very fine in your evening dress. As you would be well aware."

"That wasn't my question."

This time her eyes did not stray. Her brows pulled together as she scrutinised his face and let her gaze wander lower to his neckcloth and the sober waistcoat under the narrow-fitted coat. She blinked as she hastily drew her attention back up from his breeches. "You look what you are, Lord West. A man of means with a good tailor."

"Damned with faint praise."

CRBD

Margo blinked at the rawness of his tone. He would not have wished for her to eulogise over his appearance in the past. He had never been one to care overly about his wardrobe. He could afford the best, his fortune being large. His father had married an heiress from South Africa whose father had made his fortune in the Dutch East India Company, long before the British claimed that territory. She had bequeathed him his eyes and the jewel Margo wore at her throat. Ainsley's gift to her on her eighteenth birthday.

"I don't understand. Why are you angry?" Surely, she was the one with the right to harbour anger against him. She fingered the large tiger's eye in her pendant. It reminded her of him, the bright gold streaks in his dark eyes, pale flames in the night. *What the hand, dare seize the fire?* Did she dare reach out for what she wanted, had always wanted?

His eyes flickered as he watched her hand clutching the stone. "Why do you wear my gift?"

"It matches my dress." She spun around, letting the pale gold fabric flare out, speaking her defiance. "You see. No other reason."

"You look magnificent."

Her movement had somehow brought her closer to him. Or had he moved? His hand reached out and Margo felt the slight pressure as he stroked the stone.

"It was my mother's."

"Do you want it back?" She lifted her hands to fumble with the clasp, but he stopped her, taking her wrists, and drawing them down to rest at her waist, tangling with the satin ribbons that fell from the bow under her bodice.

"No. I don't want it back. It was a gift."

"Why did you give it to me? A family heirloom should surely stay in the family." His fingers were warm against hers, his grasp firm.

"I hoped, at the time, that you would become a part of the family."

"You..." She shook her head, hardly believing her ears. "You planned on marrying me?"

"Planned. Unfortunately, it did not eventuate."

"Because of your brother?"

He nodded. "His death changed everything. My responsibilities..."

"And a mere Miss Delancourt was no match for Lord West."

His grip tightened. "Never that."

She allowed him to draw her to the stone seat overlooking the view, keeping hold of one hand, and resting it on his knee. It was too intimate. Too everything. But she left it there all the same.

"Then why did you leave without speaking to me?"

He was silent a long moment, staring over the water. "My family have a long history of serving England. My title, Mallings, our other properties, all came as gifts from a grateful king or queen."

"I know you have an ancestor who served with Drake. There is a portrait of him in the long gallery at Mallings."

"He not only served with Drake. He spied for him, for Queen

Elizabeth. We are a family of spies, Margo."

Her heart gave a painful thump. Ainsley? In danger? "Is that where you've been all this time?"

"Once Frederick died, it was my duty to take on his obligations. I could not shirk it, for our families honour was at stake."

"It all sounds rather like a fairy-tale."

He grimaced. "No fairy-tale. It was dirty and dangerous and unpleasant. There was always a chance I would not return."

"Is Lady Gabriella a spy also?" She couldn't help the question. Envy tightened her throat at the other woman sharing his adventure.

"This is not for public consumption, Margo. People's lives may be in danger if you speak out."

"Why are you telling me this, if you do not trust me to keep silent."

He rubbed the back of his neck. "Because I hope you might have reason to keep silent."

Hope burned in her chest and she pressed hard on her bodice, the beating of her heart wild under the softness of satin and linen. "What reason?"

"Are you so blind, after all these years?"

"All I remember is you walking away, time after time. You gave me nothing to hope for."

"I gave you my pledge." He indicated the pendant. "It is the bride gift for the women of my mother's family."

"I didn't understand. You said nothing."

"I had spoken to your father, but my brother's death, so soon after my father's, complicated things."

"He said nothing to me."

"I am certain he hoped for a better match. By the time I became more than a younger son, I had to leave the country, so his hopes were dashed."

"He has quite given me up. I am to dwindle into an aunt and will spend my time travelling from sibling to sibling as they need assistance with childrearing."

"I doubt it."

Her heart gave that little skip again. "I am sure you will be off doing your duty."

"They have released me."

"Released?"

"I am permitted to return to Mallings and live the life of a bucolic landowner."

"Bucolic. I hardly think you will sink to that extreme."

His eyes burned as he leaned closer. "Who will prevent it?"

"You will find some young girl, newly out, and set up your nursery."

"Why should I put myself out, when you are right here. Margo, will you not take me seriously?"

She withdrew her hand from his clasp and pressed it against her churning stomach. "I am afraid. It hurt too much each time you left."

"I know. I am deeply sorry I put you through so much pain, but I was under oath not to share information. Not when so much hung on our discretion."

"What if we are at war again? Will you have to go?"

He shook his head. "Once I marry, I am no longer suitable. They consider love makes a man weak. He has too much to lose."

"Love?"

"I love you, Margo. Will you give me a chance to make it up to you? Show you what a life together might be."

It was hard to believe. To take him on trust and accept that he would not vanish into the night once more.

"I cannot... surely..."

He lifted the gemstone at her throat, his knuckles searing a line across the flesh revealed by her bodice. "In the east, they say the stone protects you from evil. Some say it helps with seeing the truth, to see clearly. What does it tell you?"

"It has always been a comfort to me." His warm breath caressed her cheek. He was so close, so near. So very dear. "It has brought you to my mind many times over the years."

"In anger?"

Margo shook her head. "No. More a sadness. A regret."

"You hoped for my return?"

The warmth at her throat rose higher, burning her cheeks. Surely the ruby glow of the lamp must be kind to her modesty. "We all wished you well."

"And you?"

"I hope it is well with you."

"Oh Margo. You never used to be shy."

"I have learned not to wear my heart on my sleeve."

He sobered immediately. "Did they give you a hard time, my love?"

"The first time. I did not speak of Paris once I returned."

"I am sorry for that. It was not well done of me to leave you without a word."

"I understand, now."

"I don't imagine that salves the hurt."

She looked up, meeting his gaze, seeking the familiar brightness of those tawny eyes. "You have done much to assuage my sorely bruised heart tonight."

"Do you think your father would accept a visit from me tomorrow? More importantly, would you wish me to renew my offer?"

Lowering her eyes to seek inspiration in the large oval pin at his throat, she nodded, her breath suddenly short. With a tentative hand, she reached to touch the pin. "It matches my pendant exactly."

"They are two halves of one whole. Cut from a larger stone to make a matching set. The two are meant never to be apart."

She stared at his face. "As we are?"

"Finally, you understand."

At last, she could accept his words. The pendant he'd given her all those years ago was his troth. It had simply taken longer for him to be able to fulfil the oath implicit in the gift.

"What would you have done if I had married another?"

Flames licked his gaze. "Would you have?"

"N... no." For it had been her own choice to send Seldon and all the other suitors away. The pendant had been her constant companion. Her constant hope.

His arms wrapped around her, one hand tilting her chin up. "You'll marry me?" There was an element of command in the simple question.

"Yes. Yes, I will."

His lips touched hers softly, a faint brush that prickled and burnt. "Do you love me, Margo?"

"More than life. I have loved you for such a long time, Ainsley, I had almost forgotten when it began."

Margo surrendered to the blazing heat of his kiss, fever taking hold, consuming the darkness, leaving only fire and light.

Tyger, Tyger...Burning Bright.

12

RETURN TO CRYSTAL BAY

JANE NEWTON

"Or you might like the rose quartz for its soothing and reflective properties. It opens your heart chakra so you can invite love and new relationships into your life."

Keira tried not to screw her nose up as she placed the pale pink pendant quickly back on its display stand. "No thanks."

The grey-haired shop owner smiled and the assortment of bangles on her wrist jangled as she pointed further along the counter. "I've got it—tiger's eye. It's the perfect crystal for you, sweetheart. And it's mined locally."

Keira held back an eye-roll at the endearment and the assumption that this woman knew what she needed after their three-minute acquaintance.

"And what does that one do?" She walked to where the woman had pointed and picked up the smooth, long pendant, snared in a winding silver setting. The muted gold interspersed with earthy tones certainly appealed more than pale pink. She ran a finger along the crystal, which seemed to mimic undulating waves of desert sand with raised lines hit by sunlight and others cast in afternoon shade.

"It promotes harmony, releases fear and anxiety, and helps you make rational decisions without being ruled by your emotions."

Keira nodded. "This one." She put it down while she fished in her bag for her purse. As a science teacher, she wasn't prone to magical thinking, but something about being back in Crystal Bay after being away for fifteen years caused her to channel her teenage self. Without giving it too much thought, she'd allowed nostalgia to steer her into the crystal shop she and her friends had loved browsing in on their way home from school. Back then she couldn't afford to splurge on a fifty-dollar crystal on a whim, but finally having a permanent teaching role after so many years of casual teaching meant she could now.

While waiting for the shop owner to write out a receipt, Keira turned to look out towards the headland. Maybe living back here *would* help her to feel calm and make balanced decisions without her heart getting in the way. She knew the banded crystal she'd just bought didn't have that power, but she did.

⌘

Rowan propped his board against the back of his van, towelled his hair dry and then began peeling off his surf shirt. He preferred to get in and out of the water early, before too many younger surfers inundated the waves, but he was running later than usual today and so had cut his surf short rather than doing battle with the school holiday crowd. Mitch had opened up the shop for him this morning, but Rowan needed to get there soon for the mid-morning rush.

After giving his auburn-tinged curls one last shake, he slid on a T-shirt and stowed his gear in the van. He moved towards the driver's side but then stopped dead as he caught sight of a woman walking along the esplanade. Her long dark hair was styled differently and she'd lost some of her youthful softness—now looking like someone who followed a regular and rigorous workout regime—but he would have recognised Keira anywhere.

He did a quick calculation and realised it had been more than ten years since he'd seen her. The last time had been awkward, at a party organised by their parents that they'd both attended under protest. His mum had argued it would be 'fun' to catch up with his high school girlfriend. It had been anything but. The wounds had still been too fresh.

Now, though, he was sure it would be easier to talk to her. Time and distance had numbed the hurt. He saw the moment she caught sight of him and slowed her pace. He watched as she clasped a pendant she wore around her neck and then came to a stop.

"Rowan," she said softly. "You're still living in town?"

He smiled but knew it didn't register in his eyes. Maybe talking to her wouldn't be so easy after all. "Yep," he said, aiming for a breezy tone, but realising he sounded a bit abrupt. "I bought the surf shop a few years back. I'm living in Mum's old house."

Keira lowered her gaze. "Oh, that's right. I heard she passed away. I'm so sorry."

Rowan resisted the urge to ask why Keira hadn't made it back for the funeral. He knew from her parents that she rarely came back home these days, but she'd always liked his mum. If his mother's passing hadn't been enough to draw her back, he wondered what had prompted her visit now.

Before he could ask her, she supplied the answer. "I got a permanent job at Silver Sands High. I'm staying with Mum and Dad until I work out where I'm going to live." When she caught his bemused expression, she scrunched up her nose in the same way he remembered her doing back when they were together. "I know, I couldn't get out of here fast enough after high school. And now I'm right back where I started."

The shrug she offered didn't tell him much, and neither did her explanation. He couldn't help remembering their conversations—or rather their bitter arguments—fifteen years ago. *Why do you want to stick around and rot in this backwater? Come to Perth with me. Do something with your life.*

And yet here she was. Back in the backwater. He wondered what life events had pushed her back here. Maybe she was retreating from a dissatisfying city existence, or maybe she'd simply reached an age where she wanted to be close to her parents again. Did he want to know?

Surprisingly, he found he didn't need to ponder that question for very long. "I have to get to the shop now, but would you like to catch up later? Maybe for a drink at The Hive?"

Rowan noticed the slight blush that reddened Keira's olive skin. She'd never been able to stop herself from blushing. He couldn't help wondering what it meant now. She tilted her head to one side, clearly contemplating her answer.

"Okay," she answered slowly. "Seven alright with you?"

He nodded and smiled. Watching as Keira continued along

the footpath and then crossed the road before heading down to the beach, he began to wonder if it was a mistake to arrange to meet up with her. Maybe it would have been a better strategy to duck and weave to avoid the inevitable blows.

ೲ

Keira hoped her white cotton shirt and denim skirt said casual and uncomplicated. She tucked the tiger's eye pendant under her shirt collar, hoping not to give the impression she'd become New Agey and alternative. Even so, she couldn't bring herself to take the pendant off. The words of the crystal shop owner kept echoing in her head and she couldn't help hoping that wearing the pendant would allow her to become the embodiment of calmness and rationality.

When she'd told her parents she was heading out to meet Rowan Kelly, her mother's mouth had puckered and she'd discovered a sudden need to take down and wash all the curtains in the house. Nothing had changed. Her mum had always avoided difficult emotions and preferred to bury herself in busyness. Her dad had been more supportive. *She's just worried about you, love. She remembers how you were all those years ago, when you and Rowan split up.*

She didn't need to be reminded of how fragile she'd been during her first year of uni. She'd initially brushed off Rowan's inability to put their relationship first but had eventually fallen under the weight of a crushing depression that her mother had to come to Perth to help her recover from.

Realising she was still clutching the pendant, she let it fall and then tried to draw herself up so that she was taller, tougher. She would meet Rowan and find out what path his life had taken, give him a well-edited précis of her own, and then say goodnight. This meeting was a good thing. It would mean they wouldn't have to avoid each other. If they ran into each other in town or out socially, they could say a friendly hello and move on.

Half an hour later in the beer garden of The Hive, Keira's resolve was wavering. She'd bought herself a glass of wine, so she'd have something to do while she waited. She'd forgotten how, even in holiday time, you could get from one end of Crystal Bay to the other in no time at all. After fifteen years of city traffic it was hard to break the habit of allowing extra time for every trip. She was a good ten minutes too early, so she drank the glass of wine slowly, wishing she'd ordered a beer instead.

When she finally saw Rowan, her gut roiled like the waves she could hear across the esplanade. She'd thought the second time would be easier. He was the same person, but with an extra layer of muscle and a confident air he hadn't had in his late teens or early twenties. As he made his way across the beer garden, he waved and stopped to chat to a few people he knew. People Keira might have recognised too, if she was able to look at them, but her gaze was firmly riveted on Rowan.

She saw that he held two beers and, as he sat down, he placed one on the table in front of her and sipped the other himself. "Sorry, I didn't know you already had a drink." He frowned. "And I didn't know you'd switched to drinking wine. I guess a lot can change in fifteen years."

Keira laughed nervously. "Actually, the wine is terrible. I don't know why I ordered it." She pushed the glass aside and picked up the beer instead. "Cheers."

He raised his glass and took another sip, his slate-grey eyes not leaving hers. Her breath hitched as she remembered the first time those eyes had locked on hers, when he'd asked her to dance at the year ten formal and she'd said no. And then she'd told him why—she couldn't dance despite the mandatory dance classes they'd all endured during PE—and he'd taken her behind the hall and given her a lesson, where they could still hear the music but nobody could see them. He'd been so patient and gentle.

"So are you teaching science like you always wanted to?" he asked, shaking her out of her reverie.

"I am. I've been casual or doing temp blocks for so many years. It'll be great to finally have a school to call home."

She wondered whether he'd already known the answer to that question and was just making small talk. Then again, maybe his mother had avoided talking about Keira the way her parents had resolutely avoided talking about Rowan for so many years. Just over ten years ago they'd thought she could handle seeing him again but had quickly realised she couldn't when she'd spent the rest of her visit moping around the house and periodically getting teary.

He gave her a half-smile. "Are any of our teachers still there?"

"Sazdanoff, Mitchell," she said, counting on her fingers, "Costas, Graff. Patel is the principal now. Those are the only ones left from our time."

"It was a long time ago, I guess," he said, his gaze finally sliding away from her and towards the water.

She turned her head in the same direction. The sun had already completed its fiery descent into the ocean and the red-streaked clouds glowed against a sky that was growing steadily darker. "I'm sorry," she said on a rush of breath. She hadn't realised how badly she needed to say that until the words were out.

"For what?" he asked, confusion clouding his expression.

She inhaled and exhaled slowly. "When I left, I said some things I shouldn't have. I was acting out of hurt, disappointed that you wouldn't follow me. It was silly, expecting you to give up everything and leave your family to chase after me. I understand that now."

The crease that had formed between his brows deepened. "No, it wasn't silly. I shouldn't have been afraid. I wish I'd had a more adventurous streak. But by the time I'd built up the courage to move away, I didn't think you'd ever want to see me again."

She shook her head slowly. "It was the wrong time for us. But we can put it behind us now, right? We can try to be friends again—or at least not need to run away when we see each other around town."

His frown dissolved and he smiled, the slate grey of his eyes turning softer. "Sure. I won't hide from you if you don't hide from me."

She grinned and they sat in companionable silence for a while, and then she asked, "So, the surf shop... What's running it like?"

⋘⋙

After they'd broached the subject of the past, their conversation flowed more easily, and Rowan felt himself unwinding. He talked about how he'd had to bring the surf shop out of the Dark Ages after buying it from the McKenzies. The couple had moved to Perth to be closer to their daughter and her young family. He told Keira about how he'd bought his brother out of the house after their mum died, and how he'd started to renovate it, doing a lot of the work himself to keep costs down.

She told him horror stories about some of the worst classes she'd encountered as a casual teacher.

"And they jumped out of the window and ran away?" he asked, incredulous.

She nodded and gave him a slow smile. "Five of them. And this was two months after I qualified. I had no idea what to do. I couldn't chase them and leave the other twenty-five kids in the classroom. But I couldn't let them leave school grounds."

"What did you do?"

"Called the deputy principal who said not to worry—they'd come back. And they did eventually. Except for one, who stayed outside under the window and at least listened to the lesson. I think."

Rowan raised his eyebrows and sipped his beer. "Can you imagine if we'd done something like that when we were at school?"

Keira shook her head. "Times have changed. Though I hope things haven't changed too much at Silver Sands. With any luck I won't instigate an exodus when I announce we're actually going follow structured lesson plans and not just watch movies."

"I think you'll be okay. I can't imagine Patel putting up with that. Besides, not that much has changed in Crystal Bay." He reached across the table and touched her hand, not completely sure why he was doing it. He was inextricably drawn to her. Just like he always had been. He worried she'd draw her hand away, but she didn't. Instead she met his gaze, a question in her eyes.

"I know I didn't follow you, but I never stopped thinking about you." The words were out before he could evaluate them properly, weigh them up and decide if it was wise to say them.

That familiar blush travelled quickly up Keira's face and into her cheeks. "Me neither," she whispered. "I never stopped. I tried for so long to get over you, but I'm not sure I ever did." Then she looked down at the table and laughed softly. "Bit intense for a first date, right?" She grimaced. "Not that this is a date."

Rowan placed one finger under her chin and lifted it gently so that she was looking at him again. "Maybe it could be."

A beat passed and then Keira leaned forward, reducing the distance between them by half. He tried to bite back a smile as he narrowed the gap even further. In another moment his lips were on hers. It was only a brief, soft kiss, but it felt like coming home after a prolonged absence, even though he was the one who'd never left.

When they drew apart, she grinned at him. "That's not the way I saw this going."

"Me neither," he admitted, but he was glad it had. He'd never loved anyone the way he'd loved Keira. Over the years he'd reasoned it was just because she'd been his first love, but now he knew it was because of who she was. None of those feelings had gone away. And now they had time to explore them, and the life experience to draw on if things got tough.

They talked a while longer, this time about their various relationships over the years. Both of them admitted they'd never settled on anyone because it hadn't felt like what they'd once had together.

"So tomorrow," he said later, "you want to come and see

what I've been doing with the house?"

"I'd like that."

✺

As they got ready to leave, Keira touched the pendant around her neck again. Did she want to make rational decisions without letting her emotions come into play where Rowan was concerned? Was that even possible? She watched him as he pushed in his chair and carried their glasses back to the bar, stopped to endure what appeared to be good-natured ribbing accompanied by glances in her direction from some of the people he'd spoken to earlier.

She smiled to herself and got to her feet. He'd kissed her, admitted he'd never stopped thinking about her, just as she'd never stopped thinking about him. She wasn't sure what would happen next, but she couldn't wait to find out what a future with Rowan in it might hold.

Carefully, she removed the pendant and placed it in her bag. She'd take it back tomorrow and see if she could exchange it for the rose quartz one.

13

THE FUTURE IS BEHIND YOU

PAMELA SWAIN

Rosie leant against the temporary railings and observed the queue. A group of teenage girls busied themselves pretending not to notice the boys jostling for position further down the line. But the hair flicks and whispered comments behind cupped hands betrayed them. She smiled, remembering her teenage years.

"Right. Your turn, Rosie."

Chloe, her best friend, held the tent flap open ready for Rosie to enter. "C'mon, you'll love her. She's brilliant."

"Doubt that. You realise it's just my Aunt Kath, don't you?"

Chloe nodded. "But in there she's not." She snatched hold of Rosie's hand and steered her inside the tent.

It took a few seconds for Rosie's eyes to adjust to the subdued lighting. Her nose itched from the perfume her aunt favoured. She pressed her index finger against her top lip to stem a sneeze.

Aunt Kath wafted across to her seat in a cloud of patchouli. "It's all in your mind, Rosie. And sit down. Tempus fugit. I haven't got all day."

"Excuse me?" As commanded, Rosie sat down on the chair beside her aunt.

"The answer. Grand plan. Call it what you like. I'm not going to beat about the bush, because there's a queue stretching into next week out there. Here." She pressed a gemstone into Rosie's palm. "Keep it with you always and you'll have clarity of mind... especially at sunrise during a waxing phase of the moon. Please put a donation in the charity box on your way out."

Aunt Kath dismissed her with a wave of her hand and Rosie shuffled out feeling let down, forgetting about the donation.

Chloe zoomed in on Rosie as she emerged from the tent. "Well, what did she say? She's brilliant, isn't she?"

"Hmm. Really? She didn't say much. Just gave me this." Rosie shook her head and handed the gemstone to Chloe, who held it up to the light.

"Wow. She didn't give me one. It's gorgeous. Look at the gold flashing through the brown. What is it?"

"Dunno."

"It's a tiger's eye." A deep male voice Rosie didn't recognise answered.

Both turned to stare at the owner of the voice. And who wouldn't? He was gorgeous. A good head and shoulders taller than her, with a gym toned body, a bit like Russell Crowe in his Gladiator days. He would be scary, except for the aura of gentleness shining from within him, laughter lines etched deep around his eyes. His salt and pepper hair stood in short spikes and reminded her of an echidna. She sensed he'd laugh good-naturedly if teased about it.

"And how would you know what stone it is?" Rosie cringed at the snap in her voice. The poor bloke had done nothing to warrant it. After all, he couldn't be blamed for her spineless ex's behaviour. She noticed a slight shake of his head and pictured a speech bubble above him, "*Now then, what do you make of this woman? She may be cute, but definitely a barracuda. Approach with caution. They can bite.*"

He rewarded her with a smile that reeled her in. "My sister is into gemstones and all this psychic nonsense."

"If it's nonsense, why are you in the queue?"

"A bet."

"A bet?"

"My so-called mates." He pointed towards the rifle range where two men stood, each holding teddy bears. When they noticed Rosie looking in their direction, they laughed and waved their respective bear's paws. She waved back, felt a rush of heat to her cheeks and looped her arm through Chloe's in order to drag her away.

"Well I hope the prize is worth it."

He locked eyes with Rosie for a moment too long. "Oh, it is... and I've a feeling it's already mine."

CXXO

Ben manoeuvred the chair, so the small table was between

him and the psychic. He wiped his palms along the legs of his shorts and eyed the exit numerous times. If questioned later, he doubted he'd be able to recall anything she'd said. Why was he so nervous if he didn't believe in psychic powers? Maybe his encounter with the petite redhead outside the tent had unsettled him more than he realised. Her eyes were the most amazing green he'd ever seen. Wow. And feisty. He'd irked her so much with his uninvited comments, he'd half expected her to clamp her hands on her hips and stomp a foot on the ground. But there was something about her. He sensed a vulnerability, rather like his own. He began to fidget and tapped his toe against a table leg. He had to get out. He had to find her. And then what? Ask a woman he'd spoken to for less than a minute out on a date? More like stand there spluttering and unable to form a sentence. The psychic sprang up and he almost fell off his chair. She indicated for him to hold out his hand and then pressed a tiger's eye into it.

"Keep it with you to give you confidence and optimism. The future is behind you."

Ben stood, thanked the woman, and placed $20 in the donation box on the way out. He paused at the entrance to ask her to clarify what she meant about the future but thought better of it and backed out through the flap. Straight onto the toes of the woman he'd encountered prior to entering the tent.

"Sorry. Did I hurt you? I hope ..."

"I'm okay. No damage. It was my fault, anyway. I was standing too close to the entrance." She held up the takeaway coffee cup in her hand. "I wanted to sneak in to give my aunt this before she sees the next person."

Ben stood aside for her to enter. Should he wait and offer to buy her a drink? So much for confidence boosting gemstones.

He went in search of his friends instead.

She occupied his thoughts for the rest of the night, and he found himself scanning each sideshow and ride for a glimpse of red hair. He left the showgrounds weighed down with the sense of missed opportunity, not having caught sight of her again.

❀

Rosie tossed and turned all night. She gave up on sleep just before dawn, untangled herself from the sheets, and padded downstairs to the kitchen to make coffee. She sat on the top verandah step to watch the sunrise, her hands around the mug to warm them. An autumnal nip in the air made her shiver. Her car was loaded ready for the journey north and the house-sitting stint she'd agreed to do. Couch surfing at Chloe's for a week first and then she'd be off.

Six months ago, she and her partner had been talking about it being the right time for them to start a family. The next day he'd arrived home from work, packed a suitcase, heaved it into the boot of his car and shouted that he couldn't do it anymore. She hadn't seen him since. No explanations. No phone calls. No emails. He'd left her to sell the house, pack up their belongings and arrange storage. How she wished she'd had a huge bonfire instead.

❀

Ben sprang out of bed early with the intention of finding at least one house to view. His GP position started the next week and he needed to find somewhere closer to the surgery than his sister's place. She'd offered sanctuary and a place to heal after the disaster his marriage had become—even if he did have to put up with her obsession with chakras, crystals, and gemstones. She'd been thrilled with the tiger's eye he'd been given—said it was the correct stone for him—and wanted to make a key ring of it so he'd keep it close.

He crept down the hallway, not wanting to wake her, his eyes drawn to the tiger's eye staring at him from the kitchen table. He picked it up and wandered out to the backyard, sat on a rickety bench seat, and rolled the gem between his palm and the arm of the seat. He closed his eyes and allowed the early morning sun to warm him.

Although his eyes were closed, he saw a garden dominated by a mature poinciana tree. A round swing, with a tyre rim and spider's web seat, hung from one of the branches. A child raced out from the blue door of a weatherboard house. A chocolate and white, curly coated dog followed, overtook the child, and set about digging holes in a vegetable bed. Was it a poodle? Maybe not. It looked sturdier.

"Mummy. Come and push me on the swing."

And there she was. The petite redhead, a strand of stray hair loose from her ponytail annoying her. She swatted it away from her face as she picked her way through the toys strewn about the grass.

Peals of laughter erupted as she pushed the child. "Higher. Higher. Like daddy does."

"What are you smiling at bro?"

His sister's voice pulled him back to the present. He jumped up off the seat and strode towards the house.

"Good morning to you, too. Grumpy or what?"

ೞೞ

Rosie took the winding coastal road. She opened the driver's window to savour the briny air. A whiff of old seaweed assaulted her nostrils. She knew, well before the GPS informed her, that the side road she needed would be after the next series of bends. She also knew the house would be white weatherboard with a wraparound verandah and have a blue door. But when she drove into the driveway and saw the round swing hanging beneath a poinciana tree, she slammed on the car's brakes. OMG. The swing with the spider's web seat.

She glared at the tiger's eye ring on her right ring finger and regretted asking the jeweller to make it. Once the visions began, she should have hidden it in a drawer or buried it. It was no surprise when a chocolate and white curly coated dog appeared at her side. She also knew 'The One' would appear soon.

Who he was, she couldn't say, because his face remained out of focus. But she knew her head would be just short of his shoulders and he would reach down and tilt her head up to gaze into her eyes, trace along her lips with his fingertips and smile a world of love and tenderness. She knew his lips would graze, tease her, and drive her wild with desire. And when he stood there on the doorstep for the first time, in his oil stained shirt and smudged cheeks, she would know. Know without a doubt that his arrival meant home.

ೞೞ

Rosie awoke to the sound of waves crashing onto shore. A

month ago, when she'd first arrived, the roar had kept her awake all night, but now it lulled her to sleep and eased her awake in the mornings. That and the gentle snores of the dog curled up beside her. Her attempts to find its owners had been unsuccessful. It was about time she gave him a name.

She stroked under his chin. "How about Truffle?"

The dog shot her an accusatory look.

"Well, the vet did say you were bred for truffle hunting."

He seemed to accept her logic. She showered, dressed, and settled down to complete the drawings for an ad campaign she was involved in. Truffle zoomed through the open kitchen door and deposited the ring by her feet. She'd buried it in the veggie bed the previous week. For some reason, she found herself drawing the poinciana tree and round swing with a child sitting on it, legs outstretched and head tossed back in laughter. A woman pushed the child from behind. Speech bubbles appeared above their heads. "Higher. Higher. Like daddy does." And beyond the swing, Truffle busied himself digging the veggie patch, while on the verandah, sat a man with spiky echidna hair. He held a mug with Ben written on it.

She shivered and raced off to find the trowel to rebury the ring. But this time, in one of the corrugated-metal raised beds instead.

CR80

Ben had been finding the journey tiring after long days at the surgery and needed to concentrate on his house search. He'd lined up six properties to see at the weekend. The first three were duds. On the way to the fourth property, he pulled in at a viewing spot to watch the ocean for a while. He got out of the car to stretch his legs and noticed a child racing along the water's edge, a bedraggled dog diving in and out of the waves. He scanned the beach for the petite redhead and saw her kneeling beside a lop-sided sandcastle, hands shielding her eyes from the glare as she watched her child. The child looked in his direction, performed a happy dance and raced towards the sandcastle.

"Daddy. Come and see our castle."

Ben caught sight of the tiger's eye key ring in the ignition. Its yellow stripes flashed gold.

"Today's the day then." He burst out laughing at the ludicrous way he'd spoken to the key ring. "If my patients could see me now, they'd have me committed."

He knew the woman and child would be gone from the beach when he next looked and that his car would fail to start. He could have smeared oil on his own cheeks and shirt to order, if he'd so desired, but chose to see what happened when things were left to play out unassisted. He lifted the bonnet, checked for any obvious loose caps or wires, and decided he was a better doctor than mechanic. No signal on his mobile. Damn it. He checked his reflection in the driver's mirror and burst out laughing again. *Okay, so it's a hike down that lane now then.*

He set off towards the cottage with the poinciana tree in its garden but strode straight past it and on towards the village nestled in the hillside about a kilometre away. The tiger's eye heated up in his hand until it was almost too hot to handle. He turned back, stood at the end of the driveway and stared at the place. Frozen, he clung onto the gatepost for support and fought the urge to run. Towards the village? Or the blue door? He knew, without a doubt, Rosie would be waiting the other side of that blue door. Rosie? Where had that come from? Tingles shot down his spine.

Something licked his hand and he launched several feet forward. Where had the dog appeared from? It scooted off and plunged into the raised vegetable bed, dug a hole, and stuck its nose in to retrieve something. It then came to heel and nudged his hand. A tiger's eye ring winked at him in the sunlight. Now he really was losing the plot. An inanimate object cannot wink. He patted the dog, eased the ring out of its mouth and set off along the gravel pathway.

ᖇ৪৪

Rosie glanced through the window in time to see Truffle dive into the raised vegetable bed. Damn dog. Always digging. She also saw him retrieve the ring and race off. *This is it then. He's here.* Just a matter of waiting for him to knock on the front door. She paced along the hallway, hands clamped to her chest. Who was it that said, *'Be still my beating heart?'* She leant back against the wall and closed her eyes, sighing. Footsteps crunched along the gravel pathway. She opened her eyes to check her appearance in the mirror. As usual, a stray strand of hair had escaped her ponytail. She tried to wedge it behind her ear and drew in a deep breath to calm herself. She checked her watch and then the hall clock. A moment later checked her watch again, smoothed her sweaty palms along her jeans and wondered if there was enough time to change outfits. She charged to the bathroom to get a cleaning cloth instead.

For goodness sake, pull yourself together, Rosie. She resumed taking deep breaths. And waited for that knock on the door, knowing that if it didn't happen soon, she'd fling the door open and race out to embrace him.

If only.

ᑲᔓᑐ

Ben raised his hand to knock on the door. It opened before he made contact and he almost hit her on the nose. She thrust a cloth into his hands and he passed the ring and key ring to her while he wiped his oil stained hands on the cloth.

"Two tiger's eyes, then."

"Seems like it."

"My aunt has some serious explaining to do."

"Not really. She told me my future was behind me. And it is… was."

"That doesn't make sense."

"I backed right into you… at the showgrounds, when you were waiting outside the tent. You are my future."

Ben reached to ease the stray strand of her hair away from her cheek. His fingers brushed her skin and never had anything felt so intimate to him. She reached for his hand and pressed it against her cheek.

"You need to come inside and see this."

ᑲᔓᑐ

Rosie kept hold of his hand, led him into the kitchen and pointed towards her drawing lying on the table. She loved how his eyes widened as he absorbed each detail. She knew the exact moment he'd seen his name written on the mug, because he dropped down onto a chair and shook his head in disbelief. He turned to look at her. Tears glistened in his eyes. Much like hers.

He stood, reached out to tilt her chin. She quivered in anticipation. And when his lips grazed against hers, she melted against him.

Home.

14

KIT

CHERYL BAKER

"**M**y horoscope said I'd meet a tall, dark stranger today. Looks like he's about to walk in."

At her aunt's loud whisper, Berri glanced up from the tiger's eye amulets she was sorting and followed Cora's line of sight to the store entry. A male stood in profile, holding open the door to allow their last customer of the day to exit.

Her world tilted.

She knew that face, knew the hard line of his jaw, those high cut cheekbones that hinted at his heritage. Knew his eyes would match the gold in the tiger's eye gemstone she was holding, right at that moment when sunlight catches the gem to reveal its golden, silky lustre. His eyes had always fascinated her.

Shifter eyes.

One look from under those impossibly long, dark eyelashes and women fell for Kit Tarrant.

Hard.

She'd just been one more in a long line of women who'd given him her heart. She doubted he'd have even noticed her if he hadn't fallen at her feet—literally. He'd joked that it was the hand of Fate, but she knew Fate, and Fate had sworn Kit Tarrant wasn't on her target list that night.

Berri knew she didn't fit the mould of the wealthy, willowy socialite he usually dated. She didn't play hard and fast, didn't play by their carefree rules. Not surprising that his family had wondered whether she'd cast a spell over him.

His world was far removed from hers. As his mother had pointed out, no good ever came of a shifter and witch pairing.

The smudge stick Cora had recently burned helped to conceal her presence from him. She could escape into the back room of the store and let her aunt handle him. Berri wasn't sure she was ready to face him yet.

Not with the secret she carried.

Berri placed the last amulet in the basket on the counter and took a few steps backward, passing through the beaded curtain that separated the front of the store from the back. She stilled the slight motion of the stranded beads with a wave of her hand.

"Good evening and welcome. Are you looking for anything in particular?"

Her aunt's cheerful greeting masked the compulsion lying beneath it. Few could resist the spell woven within her simple words. Cora hadn't survived centuries without safeguards in place. Those with ill intent would find themselves swiftly leaving the store, with no memory of the new age gift shop nestled in the sleepy little beachside town.

"My heart," Kit's deep voice was part rumble, part growl. "I am looking for my heart."

ભ્યૠ

Kit knew Berri was close by. His animal sensed her. After months of searching, following every little lead, he'd finally found her. There were times when he'd thought he'd lost her forever, but then his animal would pick up her trail again and they would be rushing off in a new direction. The wards she'd erected had led him on a merry chase, but they hadn't been able to sever the bond they shared.

Bond.

Mate.

From the moment they'd met, he'd known there would be no other for him. His beast had purred for her. *Purred.* Right in front of his mother.

"Foolish to lose one's heart," the woman who'd greeted him said, as she moved a trinket out of the reach of a grey cat sitting on the wide window sill. "What made you think you would find it here?"

Kit looked closer at the petite woman. Power gazed back at him from pale blue eyes in an ageless face. Her magic skittered over his skin, testing his control. There was something very familiar about the way she tilted her chin and stared him down. Berri had the same pale blue eyes, and the same expression when she challenged him.

The same *feel* to her magic.

Whomever this woman was, she was blood-kin to Berri.

Magic could be traced through bloodlines and no two bloodlines had the same magical signature.

His animal prowled beneath his skin, wanting out.

Kit tugged on the leather thong around his neck until his spiritual stone dangled in front of him. Roughly shaped, millennia-old, the tiger's eye had protected him during some of the fiercest battles between shifters and witches in centuries past. With a jerk, he ripped it from around his neck.

Magic flooded his senses, pressing against him, raising the hairs on his arms, and sending chills down his spine. His beast pushed harder for control. He held it in check. If they'd wanted to harm him, they'd have struck by now.

But this wasn't about power.

This was about trust.

"Berri holds my heart." He might be looking at his future in-law, but he was addressing Berri. "She's held it from the moment I first saw her."

A shuffle of feet sounded from the back room. Berri always forgot to hold her wards in place when she was eavesdropping. Such an endearing quality.

A slow smile spread across the woman's face, and she reached out and patted him on the arm. "You'll do nicely."

High praise indeed.

"Niece, stop pretending you're not listening and get your butt out here," she summoned Berri. "Introduce me to your man."

A squeak of indignation and Berri appeared, rubbing her jean-clad bottom. His breath caught in his throat and his beast purred at the sight of her. She was even more beautiful. Her blonde hair was pulled back in her favoured ponytail. A dash of gloss on her lips was the only makeup she wore. She was positively glowing.

And heavily pregnant. The pale pink jumper she wore clearly outlined her rounded belly.

"Not fair, Cora," Berri glared fiercely at Cora, before turning to face him. "Kit, I'd like you to meet my aunt, Cora Faerchild. Cora, Kit Tarrant. He's not staying."

"You're pregnant," Kit stated the obvious.

Berri tilted her chin. "It is no concern of yours, Kit."

"I beg to differ. The child is mine." No way was the child not his. He wanted to shout it from the roof. "Why did you not tell me? Why did you just leave? Surely you had to know I would be there for you."

"Your mother made it very clear that I am not a suitable mate for tiger-shifter royalty."

Cora snorted at Berri's comment. Kit was beginning to like Cora.

"To hell with what my mother thinks. I love you, Berri. I want you by my side, as my wife, as the mother of my children."

"Shifters and witches never work. History is filled with wars between us. Witches don't thrive under shifter rule. I can't live in your world, Kit."

"Then let me live in yours. I can run my companies from anywhere in the world. My brother, Koda, will happily step into royal duties." He moved with the speed of his animal, pulled her tight into his embrace and wrapped his arms around her. His chin rested on the top of her head. "Trust me. We can make this work."

Their baby kicked.

"If you two lovebirds will excuse me, I am going to close up shop and head to the pub for a celebratory drink." Almost before the words were spoken, Cora was shuffling them out the front door and locking it behind her. She hugged them both simultaneously. "Welcome to the family, Kit. If you want to thank me for bringing you both together, a Maserati would do nicely."

Kit wasn't sure whether Cora was kidding. No way had she brought them together. It took a lot of power to control shifter royalty. Cora wasn't that strong a witch. Was she?

Berri's horrified expression wasn't reassuring.

"Please say you didn't have anything to do with this, Cora," she called after her aunt's departing back.

CO800

Cora lit the scented candles before settling into her favourite chair. Her familiar, a grey cat with a penchant for stealing Christmas decorations, curled up at her feet. From a silk bag, she pulled out seven pieces of rose quartz and placed them at equal intervals around the crystal ball sitting in the middle of the small wooden table before her. With her index finger, she traced the rune symbols carved into its timber top, felt the familiar link to her power.

She didn't need the scented candles, rose quartz and the crystal ball to foretell the future, but people were more accepting if you used the tools of the trade. She didn't mind. They were exquisite items, and she liked the ambience they lent to the small room.

She leaned forward and stared into the crystal, letting her gaze go unfocused. You had to let go of the present to see into the future.

An image took shape. Her throat closed around a tight lump and tears pricked her eyes. Cora blew out a breath.

A soft toy tiger guarded one corner of a bassinet. Kit and Berri stood with their arms around each other's waists, looking down at their sleeping daughter.

Cora knew before the baby opened her eyes that her eyes would forever mark her. One was the gold of tiger-shifter royalty and the other, the palest blue of the Faerchild witch bloodline.

Berri placed a tiger's eye bracelet around her daughter's wrist. Warded for protection. Just in case. "Will your family accept her if she's not a pureblood?"

"My family will adore her. Our little Lily will melt their hearts. They will not be able to resist her."

"Just as I was not able to resist you? Do you think Cora...?"

Kit placed a finger across her lips, silencing her words. "You caught a tiger's eye and a man's heart. I love you."

Cora let the image fade. Berri and Kit would have their happily ever after. She might not be fairy godmother material, but she could weave a love spell with the best of them.

The bell over the door chimed. Another soul in search of love. She moved to greet her newest project.

He was tall.

He was dark.

Damn, he was drop dead gorgeous.

15

THE LETTERS

EMILY HUSSEY

The door needed a shove before it swung inwards, protesting on its hinges. A musty smell greeted Jacinta as she hesitated on the doorstep. An arm reached past her and flicked a light switch. Dim light filled the passage stretching before her. Either Cynthia had used low-wattage globes, or this one struggled through a film of dust. Perhaps both.

She blinked uncertainly as dust motes swirled before her eyes. She'd spent summer holidays here as a child, but that was long ago. Where to begin? She was conscious of the clean citrus smell of the man beside her. Soap or cologne? It cut a pleasant contrast to the mustiness.

"Would you like me to stay?" he asked. "I can call the office and tell them to re-schedule today's appointments."

"Thanks, Paul, but I'll be fine. I'll start in one room and systematically work my way through the house. I have the rest of the week to sort the contents."

"Okay, but don't hesitate to call me if you need anything. You might want this."

Taking the key he held out, Jacinta noted the smooth hands and manicured nails. Looking up, she was drawn to his eyes, illuminated by the light streaming through the open door. They were a sort of sea-green shade of blue and quite mesmerizing.

Jacinta—stop staring! She flicked him a smile of thanks and he turned towards the door. He had almost stepped out into the sunshine when he halted and turned back towards her.

"I nearly forgot. Cynthia made a specific bequest." He took a small box from his jacket pocket and held it out "She left this with us and asked that it be given to you." He gave a half-salute of farewell. "I'll leave you to it. I might drop in later to see how you're going."

This time, he did leave. Jacinta stared at the small velvet-covered box. Cynthia hadn't mentioned this. She flipped the lid open and discovered a pair of drop earrings. The bottom stone was a tiger's eye cabochon; above that, two facetted jet beads were suspended in a sterling silver and marcasite setting. The art déco design indicated the era in which the jewellery may have been made.

The earrings were lovely and very unusual. They must have held a special significance for Cynthia. What a pity she hadn't left a letter or something indicating their background or provenance. Closing the lid, Jacinta slipped the box into her bag. Time to get cracking.

She drew back the curtains in the main bedroom, coughing at the resultant cloud of dust. Opening the doors to the wardrobe, she pulled clothes off their hangers and piled them on the bed. Phew! The clothing had been shut up too long. It was all good quality, but nothing she wanted to keep. She systematically folded items and dropped them into rubbish bags. The shoes followed, sensible and comfortable. The top shelf in the wardrobe yielded hats and handbags. They joined the clothes.

A cardboard box about the size of two shoeboxes sat at the back of the shelf. Jacinta stood on tiptoes to reach it, sliding it forward to where she could grasp it properly. The box tipped over, spilling photos and letters over the floor. Jacinta knelt down, gathering up the papers. Probably it could go straight in the bin. She picked up one photo and looked at it. A group of unknown people sat around a dining table; glasses raised to the camera. Nothing was written on the back. Bin it.

As she dumped the items back in the box, she came across another photo. This time, she did recognise someone. It was Cynthia, and she was with a man. A rather handsome man. The earrings caught her eye. Cynthia wore the tiger's eye earrings.

She turned the photo over. The inscription was written in Cynthia's neat script. *Gerald and myself, New Year's Eve, 1958.* Who was Gerald? Cynthia hadn't married and had never talked about her private life. Jacinta rifled through the rest of the box. There were Christmas cards, postcards, and old theatre programs. The letters tied together in violet ribbon caught her eye. Violet had been Cynthia's favourite colour. She pulled one end of the ribbon, releasing the bow. The letters were addressed to Cynthia, and all in the same hand.

To read someone's private letters seemed intrusive, but as sole beneficiary, there was no reason why she shouldn't read them. Jacinta sank onto the bed and opened the first letter.

15/10/1958

Dear Cynthia,

Meeting you last week was an unexpected pleasure. I would never have come to Pt Reilly if the Hudsons hadn't persuaded me to join them at their beach house. I was in need of a break but was not looking for company. Muriel Hudson is not one to take no for an answer, and now I have to say I'm glad.

Can I entice you to come up to the city one weekend? South Pacific has just been released and is receiving rave reviews. We could go to dinner and then see the movie. I'm sure the Hudsons would be delighted to have you as their houseguest. I'll speak to Muriel.

Kind regards

Gerald Densley

Jacinta slipped the letter back into the envelope. *I wonder if Cynthia went to the city? Gerald looks rather nice. Did she see him again?* She glanced at her watch. There was time to read one more. She opened the next letter.

04/11/1958

Dearest Cynthia,

That music still keeps playing in my head. I really enjoyed your company this weekend. As promised, I'll try to come down again before the end of the month. The Hudsons have offered me the use of their cottage any time, provided they don't have alternative arrangements in place. It is only a day since we saw each other, but I am already missing you.

Do you think me crazy if I say that I think our meeting was destined to happen? I wish we lived closer to each other. Counting the days until we meet again.

Yours ever

Gerald

Wow. Jacinta fanned herself with the letter before placing it back in the envelope. *I wonder what happened to Gerald? Why didn't Cynthia ever mention him?* She didn't have time to ponder the question. There was still so much work to do. She left the box on the bed and dragged the rubbish bags into the passage. The lounge room was the next target.

Cynthia had never exhibited professionally but was an accomplished artist. Her paintings, mostly seascapes, hung on the walls of the house. Jacinta knew she would keep some of the artwork. Deciding which was the problem.

"Hello? Jacinta?"

Poking her head around the door of the lounge room, her heart jumped to see a figure silhouetted against the open doorway at the end of the passage.

"Feel like some lunch?" Paul held up two lunch bags. "I picked up some salad rolls. I didn't think you'd have any food here." He came down the passage, moving out of profile and into clearer visibility.

"Paul, that's so thoughtful of you. You're right — I haven't done any shopping yet. Come down to the dining room." She pointed to the piles of bagged clothing. "Mind the bags. This stuff's ready for the op shop."

"You've made some headway then."

Looking at the piles, it was stating the obvious. Jacinta didn't tell him about finding the letters. Paul might have acted for Cynthia, but this was a private matter. She cleared a space for them to sit at the table. On impulse, she pulled a couple of plates out of the selection of 'good china' that was kept in the sideboard. The company was welcome after her morning in solitude, except for the memories.

"Did you know my aunt well?" She asked after a while. "I spent a lot of time here when I was a child but, as I grew up, the contact was more sporadic, or via email."

"Dad knew her better than I did. He was her solicitor years before I joined the firm." He paused, head on one side as he considered the question. "Besides drafting and updating her will, there wasn't much she required. Occasionally a document had to be witnessed, but nothing major. In recent times, I came here to save her making the trip to the office."

He smiled, an action that lit up his entire face. "I liked her. She always had a cup of tea waiting and usually cake. She welcomed the chat, I think. She told me a bit about you. I looked forward to finally meeting you."

Jacinta blushed inwardly. *I wish she'd told me about you.* "She must have been lonely. It makes me feel guilty." Visiting her aunt was one of those things she'd meant to do, but something else always came up. "Probably a lot of her friends had moved on in one way or another."

"She attended the art group each week, but she liked to reminisce about earlier days. My father was a better-informed listener. They knew some of the same people."

There was a moment's silence. Jacinta cleared her throat

awkwardly. "I'm sorry to hear about your dad. You must miss him."

"I do, but you know — your aunt, my dad... it's not unexpected, but you just hope 'not yet'."

Cup of tea. I should offer him a cup of tea. "Would you like a cuppa? I brought some milk and basic supplies with me."

Paul stood up, brushing crumbs from his suit. "Thanks, but I'd better get back to the office and leave you to your sorting. Do you want me to drop those bags off for you?"

Jacinta brightened. "That would be really helpful. There's not much room in my small car." She grabbed one of the bags as well and followed him outside. "I appreciate all you're doing for me. Can I return the favour and invite you to dinner this evening?" *Did I really say that? I don't know much about him. What if he's not available?*

Paul shut the boot of the car and moved around to stand beside her in the driveway. He momentarily blocked the sun, making her appreciate how tall he was. "That's not necessary. I don't want to put you to any trouble."

"It's no trouble at all. I have to cook for myself so I can easily cook for two. I'll do some shopping later today." She added a persuasive tone to her voice. "I'd love to hear more about Cynthia's stories." *And if she mentioned anything about Gerald.*

"Okay." The smile illuminated his face. "I'd welcome the opportunity to become better acquainted after hearing so much about you. I'll bring the wine. I'll feel bad if I don't contribute something."

Jacinta returned inside after Paul had driven off. She should be focusing on the lounge room, but Gerald's letters drew her back to the bedroom. She told herself she would only read one

or two and would then continue sorting. She took the next
envelope from the bundle and pulled out the letter.

3/12/1958

My Darling Cynthia

*The weekend went so quickly. I hated leaving
you Sunday evening. I have been thinking about our
future options. Spending time apart is killing me, but
the alternative means either you moving to the city,
or me moving down to Pt Reilly. Darling girl, I know
you will be reluctant to leave your family, and I
understand that. I am reliant on work opportunities,
so whether I can relocate will depend on securing
suitable employment. This is presuming you would
like to see more of me. I don't want there to be any
misunderstandings. If you don't want me around,
please say so. For myself, I know I have met the
woman who I want to play an ongoing role in my
life.*

Don't leave me in suspense. Write to me soon.

With all my love,

Gerald

It was frustrating to only have access to Gerald's words.
What was Cynthia's response? Did she feel the same? Jacinta
refolded the letter and picked out their photo again from the
box. She looked at them both with fresh eyes. They were leaning
towards each other, and their body language said they were a
couple. Cynthia's hand was resting on his thigh, suggesting
intimacy. So, what had happened?

She reached for the next envelope and the pages it

contained. There was a faint woody smell to the letter. Perhaps it reflected the soap he used or the aftershave. She unfolded the letter and smoothed the creases.

22/12/1958

Cynthia Darling,

You have no idea how much your response made my heart sing. I am looking at your painting now, happy that, even though I am far from Pt Reilly, a part of it hangs on my wall. It is all the more special knowing you painted it. I feel your presence each time I look at it.

Now for my news. I've been thinking about moving to Pt Reilly permanently. You met my brother, Robert, on our last visit and he loves Pt Reilly as much as I do. Well not really as much, because for me Pt Reilly also means you. I have often spoken to Robert about branching out and establishing our own business. We would work well together. I suggested we establish a practice in Pt Reilly and he agreed! Rents would be cheap and there is no competition in the town.

My love, this means we can start to plan our lives together. I'll call you before the end of the week to let you know when I will be down next.

Love Gerald

So, Gerald was moving to Pt Reilly. What business would it have been? Jacinta pondered the issue as she folded the paper and returned it to the envelope. She glanced at her watch. There wasn't time to keep sitting here. She needed to do some more sorting and then some shopping. She retreated to the lounge room to sift through books and vinyl records, packing them into cardboard cartons.

With the boxes packed and taped, she transferred her thoughts to dinner. The supermarket was down the road and she headed there next, picking up supplies which would allow her to do a fettucine and salmon dish, with a Greek salad, and cheese and fruit to follow. It would be quick and simple.

With another carton packed, and the meal organised, Jacinta retreated to the box in the bedroom. She had time to read the last letter before Paul arrived. She pulled it from the bundle.

> *5/01/1959*
>
> *Darling Cynthia,*
>
> *I'm so pleased you like the earrings. As soon as I saw them, I thought of you. Special as they are, they are not the only item of jewellery I have in mind. Robert and I are driving down on Wednesday to complete negotiations for the lease of the new office. We have to come down and back in the one day, but can you meet me for lunch? I feel it so strongly — this is a positive sign for the rest of our lives.*
>
> *I can't wait until I see you on Wednesday.*
> *All my love,*
> *Gerald*

So that's where the tiger's eye earrings came from. Jacinta opened the box again, examining them carefully. Symbols of love and adoration. On impulse, she clipped them onto her ears. She'd never heard of an engagement, so something must have happened. Why did the letters stop?

By the time Paul arrived, wine in hand, Jacinta had tidied the dining room and set the table with Cynthia's best crockery and cutlery, along with some crystal glasses. She thought Cynthia would approve.

"I hope I'm not late? Something smells good." He proffered the bottle of wine. "Shall I open this?"

"Yes, please. I'm more than ready for a drink. I've a feeling the clean-up will take longer than I thought. I keep getting side-tracked by memories. I enjoyed staying here as a child."

"Perhaps you should stay longer," he said. "There's no rush to sell the house, is there? Nice earrings, by the way."

Paul poured the wine, and they clinked glasses. "You haven't started on this room yet." He looked around at the paintings on the wall. "This is where I usually sat with Cynthia. I always liked her paintings. My father had one as well."

They stood, admiring the artworks. "Did he?" Jacinta asked. "Cynthia must have given it to him. I don't think she ever sold her work."

"She didn't give it to him. She gave it to dad's brother, Gerald. Dad ended up with it after the accident."

A band of dread tightened around her chest. "What accident? What happened?"

Paul swirled his wine around his glass, studying it before he took a sip. "They were driving down to Pt Reilly from the city. This was when they were planning to move here and had a meeting to finalise a lease on premises they wanted to rent. There was an accident. A drunk driver cleaned them up. Gerald didn't survive."

Tears sprang to Jacinta's eyes. Cynthia must have been

devastated. No wonder she'd never married.

Paul reached out and placed his hand over hers. "Now I've upset you. It was a long time ago. I don't think anyone remembers it now. Dad still established his practice here, but it was as a sole practitioner, not in a partnership. Not until I graduated and moved back to Pt Reilly."

Jacinta blinked, clearing her eyes. "I'm okay." *I was just sad for an opportunity and a love that was lost.* She gave a reassuring smile. "Take a seat, and I'll dish up our meal."

Paul reached for the bottle of wine and topped up their glasses. "Did you know there's a cinema in town? There are some good movies on at the moment." He looked up from the task, his eyes seeking hers. "Have you ever thought about moving to Pt Reilly?"

16

TIGER LILY

FIONA MARSDEN

"**P**lease, I want you to have it."

Lily looked at the boy, and at the brooch, he'd pressed into her hand. "I can't accept it. It belongs to your family."

"Dad doesn't want it. He said he's never marrying again. That makes it mine."

"You know I'm not likely to marry you, Danny."

His fair skin flushed, accentuating the scattering of pimples on his jaw and forehead under the flop of blond hair. He was a nice-looking boy and would be a handsome man once he outgrew his adolescent awkwardness.

"I know you think I'm just a kid. But it's not about that. It's perfect for you. You love tigers, and it matches your eyes."

Lily glanced back at the pen where Rajah stalked back and forth, his amber gaze on her. "Which reminds me. It's feeding time."

"Look, just take it for now."

"I…" It was too late. The boy was already loping off and she couldn't leave her post.

She sighed and shrugged. He'd be back. He'd come most days during the summer break as if he had nothing better to do than hang out at a wildlife park. From what she'd gathered by his rambling conversations, his father worked long hours and his mother had died when he was a toddler. With no other family, it wasn't surprising he'd taken to visiting where he could be sure of getting some attention. Lily only wished he was seeing her as a mother figure. At thirty-two, she was nearly old enough to be the mother of a sixteen-year-old boy. In the meantime, she'd better lock up the brooch. If it really was a family heirloom, it was probably valuable.

◯৪৪৩

Stephen West couldn't remember the last time he'd been to a zoo. Maybe when Dan was at preschool. His son had always been fascinated by animals, bringing home strays, and collecting bugs and other creepy crawlies to terrify the long line of housekeepers over the years.

There was no-one in sight at the tiger's cage. Only a large striped beast with a suspicious golden gaze watching the families wander past and occasionally stop and stare. Most were heading home at this time of day and didn't linger. He could see why Dan was so captivated. The cat oozed power and grace as it climbed the rock at the back of the enclosure and surveyed its domain.

The tiger's attention shifted, and Stephen saw a girl enter the large enclosure from the rear. She seemed unaware of the tiger crouching above her, his inimical gaze fixed on his prey.

She was wearing the khaki uniform typical of the staff but with her black hair in a long plait down her back and her small stature, she looked like a teenager. Maybe an intern.

"Excuse me." He shifted along the barrier, trying to capture her attention. The tiger was creeping forward on the rock as she approached with a large plastic bucket.

At the last minute, she looked up as the tiger sprang, landing in front of her. He reared up, and the two rolled onto the grassed area. Shock kept Stephen frozen for a moment, but then she laughed. *Laughed*.

Fear turned to anger as he took his finger off the speed dial for emergency services. "Are you some kind of idiot?"

Both the big cat and the girl looked up. Surprise stilled the clamour of his heart as he took in the two pairs of golden eyes. *Tiger eyes*. How ironic.

With a low command to the animal, the girl approached the double fence that kept the prey safe from the predator. Under that bright gaze, he wasn't sure which he was.

"I'm sorry if you were startled. Rajah is quite safe with me. I've known him from a cub."

She looked older now, an air of maturity settling over her with the obvious authority she carried.

"Does he do that often?"

Her smile was lovely, her teeth white against the dusky pink of her lips. "Now and then. It's a game."

"Is it wise to tempt the tiger?"

She indicated the bucket being investigated by the big cat. "He's more interested in the prime steak I was bringing than taking a piece out of me. He's lazy."

Stephen dragged his attention from the savage way the cat was tearing into the meat. He wasn't here for the animals. "Rajah?"

The woman nodded. "He's an Indian tiger. He arrived here as a cub and the zoo held a competition to name him."

"Are you Lily?"

Her eyes widened. The brown irises flecked with amber under the long black lashes. "Do I know you?"

"No. But you know my son."

 C380

Lily stared at the man who'd fathered Daniel West. She'd expected someone older, not a man still in the prime of life. For all his hours in the boardroom, he'd certainly managed to maintain his fitness. He was as dark as the boy was fair, his ebony hair cropped close to his scalp and heavy straight eyebrows that glowered over pale eyes.

"You've come for the brooch?"

"Are you surprised? It's a family heirloom that dates to the eighteenth century."

She drew herself up, wishing she was on higher ground. He was so tall, and the enclosure was lower than the pedestrian paths. "I had no intention of keeping it. I would have returned it next time Danny came to visit."

Those eyebrows thickened onto one straight line. "You expect me to believe that?"

"I have a well-paying job. I don't need to steal your family trinkets."

He seemed to expand, his broad shoulders in the grey suit shifting and rolling. "What about the boy? What would a woman your age want with a teenager?"

"I talk to visitors all the time, it's part of my job. Maybe if you spent more time with him, he wouldn't feel the need to spend his afternoons talking to strangers."

For a moment she was glad of the fences between them, and then he seemed to collapse with a huff of air.

"I'm sorry. This isn't your problem. Dan said he'd given it to you and I guess I assumed the worst."

"I can return it to you. It's in my locker, which is quite secure."

He glanced at his watch. One of those thin expensive ones, probably made of platinum. "When do you get off work? I'd like to talk to you."

"We close in fifteen minutes. I'll be all finished in about half an hour. I could meet you at the gate."

He nodded and turned immediately to walk away. He didn't waste words. But he certainly looked good. Mr West strode toward the exit like he owned the place, looking neither left nor right at the animal exhibits.

Lily responded to a rumble from Rajah. "You like him too? I suspect you both have a lot in common. Lord of your domain and all that."

ଔଞ୍ଚ

Stephen uncoiled himself from the seat outside the entrance to the zoo as the woman exited through a small gate to the right of the main entrance. She'd changed out of her uniform into a pair of cotton trousers and a t-shirt that left a strip of warm brown flesh exposed at her midriff. Now he could see the attraction that had ensnared his son. He hadn't given much thought to it at the tiger's cage, still reeling from the shock of that first moment of perceived danger.

Now, without the bulky khaki shirt and shorts with the heavy boots, she looked feminine and appealing with a nice amount of curve for her slight build.

Her eyes brightened as she spotted him, hurrying across the pavement, her hand rummaging in her bag. "I have your brooch."

"Later." He ran his fingers through his hair, suddenly nervous. "Look, do you have time to come and have a coffee? I haven't eaten all day."

"Sure. Where do you want to go? The café inside is closed."

"There's a place a few blocks away. We could go in my car, or you could follow me in yours."

"I'm strictly on public transport. I don't have a car."

"I could drop you home later."

She seemed unsure, and he rushed into speech as he pulled his wallet out of his jacket. "You can call someone to tell them where you are if that makes you more comfortable. This is my card."

ೞೞ

Lily took the card and studied it. Stephen West. Apart from the name, the only other thing on the glossy white rectangle was a phone number. She snapped a photo with her iPhone and handed it back. "That will be in the cloud, so if I go missing, someone will be able to track you down."

He frowned as if offended, and she let herself smile. His eyes widened, fixed on her mouth, the slight curve of his mouth a sudden jolt to her heart. He should smile more often.

"I'll keep that in mind should I decide on a nefarious purpose."

"Nefarious? That sounds rather disturbing."

The smile was everything she'd hoped for. The resemblance to his son was clear at that moment. The mother must have been fair, to give the boy such different colouring.

He led the way to a short-term parking slot and opened the door of a dark coloured BMW. Lovely manners. Another thing his son had from him.

"Thanks." She smoothed her palms over the soft cream leather, inhaling the scent of leather and something else. When he joined her in the car, she recognised it as him. A bitey aftershave with citrus elements over something musky. It was delicious, and she breathed in deeply, for the joy of tasting it all over again. She really needed to do something about the drought in her social life.

She liked the way he drove, his hands resting lightly on the steering wheel, not accelerating hard and being heavy on the brakes to show off a powerful vehicle. He was also silent, focussing on the road and only glancing her way the once, as they pulled over into a park near a small cluster of businesses. For some reason, that piqued her pride.

The café was really more a boutique restaurant, tiny but already busy with people eating pizza and pasta as indicated by the sign above the door. Probably catering to the after-work crowd. Which was good, because she didn't feel underdressed among the casually dressed and work suited diners.

A middle-aged man approached them with a smile of recognition for Stephen West and guided them to a small table towards the rear of the restaurant. To her surprise, it overlooked a small courtyard where a family group were seated.

"This is a nice place. You must come here often, Mr West."

"Stephen, please. Mr West makes me feel like a grandfather. You haven't eaten here?"

"I live in the other direction, and I guess I tend to eat closer to home."

A waitress came and took their order. Lily was persuaded into a bowl of pasta, which would save her cooking something when she went home.

Finally, they were alone, for all intents and purposes, food on the table and their fellow diners oblivious to everyone else. Even so, Stephen seemed reluctant to bring up the topic of why they were here.

"How can I help you, Mr...?" He cast her a warning glance, "I mean Stephen."

"I'm worried about Dan. He seems to be particularly attached to you. I didn't realise how often he'd been coming to the zoo until I noticed that the brooch was missing and asked him about it."

"It's been two or three times a week. He doesn't come on weekends and I'm not on duty every weekday."

"Does he interfere with your work?"

Lily shrugged, poking at the pasta. "Not really. He waits until after I finish with the public duties." She smiled down at the plate. "Sometimes he asks questions at the group sessions when he knows the small fry are too shy to speak up."

He sat back. His meal hardly touched. "You know he has a crush on you."

"It's about the attention. It's school holidays, so he's missing his friends and you're at work. He's lonely."

His long fingers dug through his short hair, spiking it up and then smoothing it down. "I've got time off next week. Do you think he'll resent not being able to come visit?"

"He knows I won't be at work, so it shouldn't be a problem."

"You're leaving?" His brows rose, wrinkling his forehead and making him seem his age, which must be close to forty.

"On holiday. I'll be out of town. I'm heading up to the north coast."

"I was lucky to catch you, in that case."

Rummaging in her bag, Lily brought out a small parcel. "I'd better give you this before I forget." Not that he was likely to forget.

He took it and unwrapped the tissue, settling the brooch on his palm. It was beautiful, an oval cut tiger's eye bound in gold that reflected the bright streaks of amber in the stone. She felt a twinge of regret that something so beautiful was not for her.

"It's a lovely specimen. You said it had a history."

His glance up was brooding, seeming to linger on her face. Heat warmed the skin at her throat.

"It wasn't always a brooch. When it first came into the family in the late seventeen-hundreds, it was part of a set - a pendant on a gold chain, and this was a matching tie pin. They were cut from a single stone and set for the bride and groom of that time."

"What a fascinating story. Do you still have the set?"

"No. The pendant stayed in England and the pin came out to Australia early last century with a younger son. By then it had been turned into a brooch for a lady."

"Fashions change."

He fingered the stone. "Even now, brooches aren't all that fashionable. My wife never wore it."

"She didn't like it?"

"Sylvia was very fair, like Dan. She said it didn't match anything she wore."

"A pity to have it sitting in a drawer or a safe."

"I guess that's why Dan thought he could give it away."

"He said you weren't ever going to marry again. If it was his inheritance, he could do what he wanted with it."

His gaze was intent. "And you agreed?"

"Of course not. He ran off before I could hand it back." She hesitated and plunged in. "Is it true? That you don't intend to marry again?"

"Are you offering?"

Her skin flushed again at his sarcastic tone. "Don't be ridiculous. I'm a stranger."

"Not to Dan. He thinks you're the best thing he's ever seen." The brooding look was back on his face, lengthening the line of the jaw and hollowing his cheeks.

"It's only because he's lonely."

"I never wanted to marry again. Sylvia was... not happy with being a wife."

"She wanted a career?"

"God no. Unless spending money was her idea of a career." He grimaced. "Not her fault. She grew up with very little. A wealthy marriage was the ultimate ambition. We didn't plan on having children straight away, so Dan was a nasty shock. She fell off a balcony at a party when he was two. I wasn't there."

Lily wanted to hug him. He was not a man to countenance failure, and he clearly felt he'd failed his wife. "You've done well. Dan's a nice lad."

"But lonely, as you keep pointing out."

"School will be back soon."

"And in another couple of years, he'll be gone."

"Will you be lonely?" It was an odd question to ask a stranger. Intrusive. Yet he didn't balk at the query.

"Perhaps. I don't have a lot of time for a social life."

"Maybe you'll meet someone on holidays. It happens."

He tucked the brooch into his jacket pocket. "Anything is possible."

There was an air of decision about him that hadn't been

there at the beginning of the evening. She gathered her things together. "Thanks for the meal. I hope things work out for you."

He took her hand, his grip warm and firm on hers. "Thank you. I think, I hope, they will."

∽∝

Stephen watched as Dan hit the volleyball over the net, pounding it into the sand before the opposition could prevent contact. It had been a good decision to come to the beach. It was a family resort town and Dan had connected with a mixed group around his own age on the second day.

He moved away, striding over the hardpacked sand. Dan would be fine for an hour or two and he had a rendezvous with the future. Somehow, the all-important business world had retreated this past few days.

She was waiting on the foreshore in front of the small bungalow he'd sought out on the third day of the holiday. Her slight figure was browner than ever in the tiger print bikini top and sarong tied low on her hips. A wide smile showed off her lovely mouth and she'd propped her sunglasses on top of her flowing black hair. He never got used to the warmth in those magnificent eyes.

"Hey, Lily."

"You're early."

"Dan is spending the afternoon with friends, so I'm free." She'd insisted he spend much of the time with his son, to rebuild their relationship. But she was always waiting for him as if she knew when he was coming.

"Come inside."

He followed her in, savouring the warmth of the welcome she gave him. Her arms opened wide, and he took the invitation, wrapping her in his embrace. No longer lonely, no long estranged from his son. His Tiger Lily had changed everything. Perhaps there was something in the family legend of the tiger's eye bringing true love. The brooch had found its way home after all.

SPICY BITES

Want to try something a little spicier?

Why not try our Spicy Bites Anthology?

Spicy Bites 2019:

Masks

Spicy Bites anthologies can be purchased from the
Romance Writers of Australia store

http://romanceaustralia.com/shop/

COMING IN **2020**

In 2020 we are refreshing the Little Gems to a new anthology brand of

Sweet Treats

Think of all those yummy treats that make you feel good, or that you might get or make for your loved ones.

The theme for 2020 is

Cupcakes

All of the terms and conditions for Sweet Treats will remain the same as they have been for Little Gems, with full details found on the Romance Writers of Australia website

https://romanceaustralia.com/contests-overview/sweet-treats-anthology/

Previous Little Gems anthologies can be purchased from the Romance Writers of Australia store

https://romanceaustralia.com/shop/

ABOUT THE AUTHORS

Chelsea Locke

For many years, I bored all my friends, saying that one day I would write a romance novel.

When I finished work, it was time to stop annoying people and write. This short story 'One and Done' came about via two OWL courses I participated in and becoming confident with my writer's voice.

In the process of developing this short story, I learnt the fun of writing the first draft, the agony of editing and deleting in the second draft and finally the quest for perfection in the third draft and knowing when to stop!

I hope you enjoyed Mike's wooing of Jane.

Hollee Mands

Hollee Mands used to be that kid who sat at the back of the class, scribbling stories, and doodling in dreary math workbooks. Much older and still unrepentant, she's now determined to bring her imagination to life on the keyboard.

When she isn't squirrelling away time to write, read or sketch — she is a communications consultant, wife and proud mom to a tiny dictator who has the speech patterns (and physical energy) to rival a steam train. 'Wanderer' is her first romantic short story.

Connect with her at https://www.holleemands.com

Lisa Stanbridge

Lisa has had a passion for writing ever since she could string sentences on a page. It began with princesses in towers being rescued by handsome princes before evolving into angsty teenagers with crushes on high school jocks.

Now, as a semi-mature adult, she writes contemporary and sweet romances.

She lives in Adelaide with her multitude of teddies, and her English husband who detests the heat. When she's not writing, she's reading, binging on Netflix, playing Sims, or re-enacting her latest novel scene with her husband, while trying not to concuss him in the process.

Sue-Ellen Pashley

Sue-Ellen is an international author with three published stories: *Aquila, When Henry Met Gina* and *Streamer,* with her children's picture book, *The Jacket*, released in May 2019. From being an avid reader and writer as a child to studying literature at university, she's always loved the written word and where it can transport her.

In her 'other' life, Sue-Ellen is a social worker, counselling all ages, including children, where stories are an important part of her work. She lives in Central Queensland with her family and a menagerie of animals, including snakes, turtles and lizards.

Suzie Jay

Suzie Jay is an Adelaide author who grew up within walking distance of the beach, dreaming of life as a famous author or Johnny Farnham's backup singer.

After a stint as a teacher and then a stay at home mum to six children, she decided to make her dream a reality. Writing romance, not singing, because she can't hold a tune and she's pretty sure she's tone deaf.

Suzie didn't give up on Johnny all together though, and in her spare time, she still sings along to 80's hits, bakes, and binges on Netflix with her own knight in shining armour- who's more likely to wear tattered footy jumpers than chain mail.

Maryanne Ross

Maryanne Ross works as a speechwriter for a major Aboriginal organisation and previously did media and communications for Parks Victoria. She loves writing fiction and has switched from writing crime to romance because the stories are so much happier. She is excited to be part of 2019 Little Gems.

Her stories have won the 2016 Thunderbolt Prize for Crime Writing, the 2017 Scarlet Stiletto 'Kerry Greenwood' award and placed in the 2017 Southern Cross Literary Competition. She has been anthologised in 2017 Award Winning Australian Writing and Scarlet Stiletto: Ninth Cut. Maryanne is currently writing an Australian historical romance.

Caroline Deness

Caroline loves romance, humour and 'happily ever afters': a relaxing contrast to her usual life as a GP. It turns out there are only so many times a year you can reread Georgette Heyer or Jane Austen. When her new favourite author wouldn't release another book for almost a year, she was forced to start writing her own!

From there, it was contemporary adventure romance; perfect when she discovered Little Gems through RWA. Even more perfect when she found modern Regency Romance. So third time lucky and a big thank you to my 'avid readers of the genre'. www.carolinedeness.com

Dianne Inglis

Dianne Inglis has dabbled with writing for years, continually promising to become more focused!

Having not one, but two competition entries in different genres successful this year has affirmed what friends and family have been telling her for years; she can write.

They have sworn to hold her to account without reprieve until she delivers the goods and completes some of her numerous manuscripts.

Stella Quinn

Stella Quinn believes romance, adventure and escape are the reasons we love to read. They're also the reasons she loves to write.

She's just finished her holiday romance series: *Tropic Storm*, *Stowaway*, which came second in the RWA Emerald Award for best unpublished manuscript in 2018, and *Island Fling*, which won the coveted Valerie Parv Award in 2018. Her novella, *The Umbrella Diaries*, is being published in Literary Crush Publishing's 2019 *April Showers* anthology, and she has another Little Gem out there in the wild, *Beneath The Waves*.

You can find and follow Stella Quinn via her website at www.stellaquinnauthor.com

Fiona Greene

Fiona Greene loves romance – reading it, and now writing it. Her works range from contemporary stories with strong heroines and even stronger heroes, to journeys across time and space, exploring the universe, one romance at a time.

Fiona lives in Brisbane, Australia.

You can find her online at

http://www.fionagreene.weebly.com

Fiona Marsden

Fiona Marsden started out as an avid reader. She was a late starter in finding romance novels, but once found, they became an addiction. It was only logical that the next step would be to write her own romances. She lives on a small rural property shared with families of kangaroos and wallabies, native birds, a koala and the odd possum, along with thousands of books, mostly romance.

A recent Release is "Tell Me No Lies." 2019. Find her on Social Media as @FionaMMarsden or on FB as Fiona Marsden Writer.

More about Fiona can be found on her website. www.fionamarsden.com

Jane Newton

Jane Newton is an avid romance reader. She's also an editor who has had the privilege of helping many authors polish their fiction manuscripts. When she can, she writes stories of her own. *Return to Crystal Bay* is her third published romantic short story and she's thrilled to be part of the 2019 Little Gems Anthology.

She's currently working on her second full-length sweet romance. When not reading, editing or writing, Jane enjoys spending time with family, taking dance classes, and taking quick walks through suburbia.

Pamela Swain

Pam lives on the Fraser Coast, Queensland, where one day is sunny and the next, a sauna. Her Russian Blue cat, Anastasia, allows Pam and her ace tea making husband to share her home, so long as she remains the only princess.

When she's not writing, Pam follows her other passions - whale watching from July to November, where seeds of stories often grow, and attending to her rapidly multiplying raised veggie beds, where she nurtures her asparagus crowns all year round. Although don't mention crowns to her cat, who has enough airs and graces already.

Cheryl Baker

Welcome to my world filled with shifters, dragons, witches, demons, and angels. Throw in an immortal guardian (or five), a kickass heroine and, of course, a happy ever after. I am a New Zealand born Australian writer of paranormal romance and have been a member of Romance Writers of Australia for over 10 years.

In 2018 I was delighted to place Third in The Emily for my paranormal romance, *Fire and Ice*. My short story *How To Tame a Dragon* is in the 2013 Sapphire Little Gems anthology and *Kit* is in 2019 Tiger's eye Little Gems anthology.

Emily Hussey

Currently working and living in Melbourne, Emily Hussey has had a varied career. She built modular houses in Central Australia, opened various businesses, and was involved in the development of Sydney Airport.

She is a published romance writer, and loves the short story format in a range of genres. She was published in the 2016 Little Gems anthology, and has been published in Stringybark anthologies. She was shortlisted in the 2018 Scarlet Stiletto Award, run by Sisters in Crime.